Sketching the Adirondacks

T.1. Jervis McEntee, ca. 1874.
Courtesy of the Sawyer Family
Collection.

T.2. Joseph Tubby, Parkinson's
Studio, ca. 1885. Joseph Tubby
Papers, 1851–88. Courtesy
of the Archives of American
Art, Smithsonian Institution,
Washington, DC.

Sketching the
Adirondacks
Letters from the Wilderness

Edward I. Pitts

Including observations of Smith's Lake, Raquette Lake, and the
High Peaks and encounters with famous guides, hermits, settlers,
and sportsmen, with illustrations by Jervis McEntee

Accompanied by explanatory notes by the author

Syracuse University Press

For a listing of books published and distributed by Syracuse University Press, visit https://press.syr.edu.

ISBN: 9780815611769 (paperback)
       9780815657415 (e-book)

Library of Congress Cataloging in Publication Control Number: 2024058830

Contents

Illustrations and Maps

Maps

Preface

This book tells a remarkable story that has largely been overlooked for almost 175 years. In the summer of 1851, two young artists, Jervis McEntee and Joseph Tubby, both still in their twenties, traveled to the central Adirondack wilderness seeking beautiful scenes to sketch. They hiked, paddled, and occasionally rode in wagons from Lowville, New York, in the Black River Valley to the Schroon River at what is now the village of North Hudson, New York. The trip took a bit more than two months and covered a distance of about 170 miles, not counting their major side trips. This book is the first full account of that trip ever published.

A detailed record of the trip exists in a daily journal kept by McEntee. The original handwritten journal and a typed transcription of it are in the collection of the research library of The Adirondack Experience, The Museum on Blue Mountain Lake, Blue Mountain Lake, New York. Copies of both items are also in the Jervis McEntee Papers, 1796, 1848–1905, in the Archives of American Art at the Smithsonian Institution, Washington, DC. This journal was unknown outside of McEntee's family and close friends until it was discovered in 1964 among papers preserved by Joseph Tubby's daughter, Gertrude Tubby.

I first learned of the existence of the journal by lucky accident. A few years back while I was doing research on other early recreational visitors to the central Adirondacks, a colleague happened to ask me whether I knew about the McEntee trip journal. I confessed that I had never even heard of McEntee. My friend explained that McEntee was a distinguished artist of the Hudson River School and that his sketching trip in 1851 was one of the earliest trips to the central Adirondacks made primarily for artistic inspiration. I was hooked. I asked my friend where I could find a copy of the journal. She told me that she happened to have a digital copy of the transcript that she would send to me. I read it a few days later.

One of the most compelling aspects of the journal is McEntee's poetic descriptions of the Adirondack wilderness. When he made his trip, much of the territory he visited had not yet been transformed from its natural state. To be sure, there were some scattered settlements and some logging and mining, but much of the wilderness remained unscathed.

Another interesting aspect of the journal is its detailed description of the daily activities of their guide, Asa Puffer. Much has been written about the exploits of other Adirondack guides, but the journal makes it abundantly clear just how indispensable a guide was for early tourists. It contains convincing details of Puffer's almost unimaginable physical strength as he walked and paddled great distances and, when necessary, pulled heavy boats up rapids. Puffer carried most of the gear, did most of the hunting and fishing, located campsites, cooked the meals, and found the trail. He rarely complained.

Unlike other accounts of trips to the Adirondacks before the Civil War, McEntee's journal also provides details of what a sketching trip of that era involved. It discusses the artists' search for suitable scenes to sketch. It records a bit about the art supplies they carried and notes the amount of time it took to create their sketches. It even records a story told to McEntee by a famous guide that humorously illustrates what locals thought about visiting artists.

After reading through the journal a second time, I was convinced that the story of the trip deserved to be more widely known. My first impulse was to find a way to publish it as it is. On further consideration, however, I realized that although some historians would find such a book interesting, the average reader attracted to Adirondack history or the Hudson River School of landscape painting would find reading a transcript rough going.

Properly understanding McEntee's journal entries is difficult. Observations of great interest and poetic beauty are mixed with mundane details about what they ate or the weather. McEntee clearly did not intend for the public to read his journal; rather, he meant to use it as a memory aid. Because of this intention, the journal omits much of the information needed to understand it. Reading it requires a great deal of patience, a willingness to wade through his archaic style, and a thorough knowledge of Adirondack history for the years preceding the Civil War.

To overcome these difficulties, I initially considered simply adding footnotes to a corrected transcript of the journal to clarify items and thus provide necessary context. I worked my way through the journal, marking every item that deserved a footnote. It soon became obvious that the footnotes would likely be as long as or possibly longer than the text they explain. The result would be an awkward and unreadable tangle.

It then occurred to me that it would be possible to extract selected passages from the journal that contain the central elements of the story and insert explanatory footnotes. I created this version of the journal by editing the daily entries, dividing the trip into three parts, each with an explanatory map, and adding the footnotes. This version was an improvement but was still difficult to follow, somewhat repetitive, and very long.

As I worked on that version, I became convinced that there had to be a better way to effectively present the most important observations contained in McEntee's trip journal. Unfortunately, strictly retaining the structure of a daily journal did not lend itself to coherently telling the story of the sketching trip.

As I reread the journal hoping for inspiration, I suddenly realized that it suggested a solution to the problem of an effective story structure. During the trip, whenever McEntee and Tubby had the time, they wrote letters to their families and friends. McEntee's journal records that he wrote dozens of such letters. Where the journal omits context, the letters would necessarily include enough for the recipients to understand the events being described.

With that in mind, I began to search for any surviving letters written by either McEntee or Tubby during the sketching trip. The

Archives of American Art at the Smithsonian Institution has a substantial collection of miscellaneous manuscripts and ephemera from both artists. The Jervis McEntee Papers are quite a large collection, but although they contain many letters that he wrote, none of them was written during 1851. None of McEntee's letters even mentions the trip.[1] The Joseph Tubby Papers, however, include two letters Tubby wrote during the sketching trip.[2] The first, written in July 1851 at Raquette Lake, describes the difficult journey from Smith's Lake to the Shingle Shanty. A second letter, written in August 1851 from the Upper Adirondac Iron Works, is addressed to Robert Grosman, a mutual friend in Kingston, New York. Unfortunately, the ink is badly faded, and the letter is mostly illegible. A partial transcript published to accompany an exhibit of Tubby's paintings reveals the letter simply mentions the same information discussed in greater detail in McEntee's journal. Tubby's Shingle Shanty letter, however, provides a tantalizing glimpse into the reality of the trip.

Absent the survival of any other letters about the trip by either artist, I couldn't help but wonder what those letters might have said. That's when I decided to try to draft a series of letters drawing their substance from passages in McEntee's trip journal. After creating a draft of letters covering the first part of the trip, I prevailed on a few friends to provide honest feedback on my approach. All of my first readers encouraged me to continue.

My next step was to collect and read everything I could find about McEntee and Tubby. A list of the sources I consulted appears at the end of this book. Although I hoped to discover more material about the sketching trip, there was not much to find. As will be detailed later, McEntee wrote two letters to local newspapers containing accounts of the first part of the trip, and eight years after the trip he anonymously published a lightly fictionalized account of the entire trip in an

1. Jervis McEntee Papers, 1796, 1848–1905, Archives of American Art, Smithsonian Institution, Washington, DC.

2. Joseph Tubby Papers, 1851–1888, microfilm roll 9, frames 339–561, Archives of American Art, Smithsonian Institution.

illustrated magazine. With all of this in hand, I set about creating the series of letters that appear in this book. I think of the result as a sort of translation or reformatting of McEntee's trip journal and related writing. Where the journal can be fragmentary and opaque, the letters constitute a coherent, readable story.

To provide the necessary background and context to decode McEntee's journal entries, I also created explanatory notes to accompany each letter. These notes provide further information on the people and places mentioned. They also include references to the source material and indicate any items of speculation.

Although McEntee's journal records that he wrote many letters during the trip, it does not reveal to whom those letters were addressed. To include as much credible context as possible, therefore, I chose to address McEntee's supposed letters to his family members and people he knew. The core events of the journey are contained in the letters addressed to McEntee's parents. Letters concerning the scenes he sketched are addressed to artists, primarily his cousin Julia McEntee; Frederic E. Church, his mentor; and Calvert Vaux, an architect and future brother-in-law. Letters concerning the guides he met are addressed mostly to his younger sister Augusta, but there's also one to his sister Mary. Poetic letters about his feelings are addressed to Anna Gertrude Sawyer, whom he would later marry. Letters describing his hiking and climbing experiences are addressed to Nathaniel B. Sylvester, an attorney who likely assisted in planning the trip.

I initially intended to include letters that might have been written by Tubby. Such letters turned out not to be feasible because of a lack of original sources. Fortunately, I was able to locate Tubby's letter to his family describing the day they traveled from Smith's Lake to the Shingle Shanty. I have included a complete transcription of it as letter 13 in this book. It is particularly interesting because it contrasts markedly with McEntee's style while remaining faithful to the events as set forth in McEntee's journal.

The resulting book of letters and notes can best be described as a work of creative nonfiction. This type of writing applies literary techniques to a subject to craft a compelling story. The primary literary technique I used in crafting these letters is writing in another person's voice. To do this convincingly and ethically, I adopted so far as possible McEntee's prose style and carefully avoided including terms and expressions not in use during the time of the trip. I also left out some but not all currently standard punctuation to reflect the style in his journal and the casual style of letters. To create a narrative trajectory, I edited out extraneous parts of the journal entries, but the resulting letters remain faithful to the facts of the trip as set forth in McEntee's writing. The notes to the letters point out the few instances where support for statements in the letters is based on my reasonable assumptions. I believe the resulting story is essentially the same one that McEntee would have told to his family and friends.

Although I created the letters in this book, they are not the products of my imagination. I fashioned the letters by meticulously extracting the facts as set forth in McEntee's trip journal, newspaper articles, and magazine article. I have added some minor elements to each letter to flesh out the story. In my attempt to evoke McEntee's style of writing, most letters include iconic phrases and excerpts from his journal. The longer verbatim journal excerpts are indicated by use of quotation marks.

The book in your hands is the result. The letters recount the story of two young artists on a quest to discover and sketch beautiful wilderness scenes. Their primarily artistic goal sets this book apart from other accounts of early Adirondack journeys. The notes accompanying the letters provide an in-depth view of conditions in the central Adirondacks in the year 1851. They also give an account of some of the issues important to American landscape painters of the time. Accordingly, this book should appeal to readers interested in discovering a new facet of Adirondack history and learning something new about Jervis McEntee, Joseph Tubby, and the Hudson River School of landscape painting.

Introduction

When their rowboat became stuck on a submerged log, Joseph Tubby stepped out of the boat into what he thought was about six or eight inches of water. He immediately sank to his waist in odorous, mucky silt. At the oars, his friend Jervis McEntee nearly split his sides with laughter. Joe laughed, too, especially when he realized that Jerv would soon have to join him in the mud to help work the boat free.

They were already soaked. It was raining hard. There were clouds of hungry black flies around their heads. They had been rowing up the twisting Shingle Shanty Brook all afternoon. They were tired, and they were sure they were lost. It was starting to get dark when they pulled their boat onto the shore next to where Asa Puffer, their guide, had beached his. Puffer tried to assure them that a road lay about a mile south through a swamp. They had become disoriented and argued with their guide about the right direction until he pulled out a compass. They picked up their sketching boxes and started walking.

It was Thursday, July 3, 1851. The two young men had completed only three weeks of a planned two-month trek across the central Adirondacks. They would eventually walk 82 miles, travel by rowboat for 58 miles, and ride a lumber wagon for the last 30 miles—a trip of 170 miles through rough, mostly unsettled wilderness.

Jervis McEntee was twenty-three years old. His longtime friend Joseph Tubby was twenty-nine. They were aspiring landscape artists from the village of Rondout near Kingston, New York, in the Hudson Valley. They had little camping experience, but they were young and determined. Both believed that a sketching trip in the wilderness would help them prove to themselves and to the art world that they should be taken seriously as artists.

This book will allow you to travel along on their adventurous journey. During the trip, they ascended the Beaver River to its headwaters at Lake Lila, then called Smith's Lake. They subsequently explored Brandreth Lake, Raquette Lake, the Marion River, Blue Mountain Lake, Long Lake, and the High Peaks. They climbed Blue Mountain and Mount Marcy and sketched at the Indian Pass. They met every working Adirondack guide of those times as well as many early settlers, hermits, and, surprisingly, other travelers.

Finding Beauty in the Adirondack Wilderness

The plan to take the Adirondack sketching trip described in this book was formed in the winter of 1850. During that winter, Jervis McEntee studied painting with Frederic Edwin Church, then a young rising star among American landscape painters. Church was one of the few painters to have studied directly with Thomas Cole, whose work and ideas had already inspired a new movement of landscape painting that celebrated America's natural world.

McEntee rented a studio for the winter near Church's studio in the American Art-Union Building in New York City. When he told his artist friend Joe Tubby about his plan, Tubby asked if he could share the studio and help pay the rent. Even though Tubby was already working in his father's construction business as a house painter, the chance to spend several months during the slow winter season devoting himself to art was an opportunity he did not want to miss. So the two of them, along with another young artist named Frank Carpenter, moved into the studio in New York to pursue their artistic dreams. It was a pivotal decision.

McEntee spent many hours that winter in Church's studio serving as his apprentice. This would have included a variety of tasks, such as preparing canvases, cleaning brushes, and the like, but it would also have involved a lot of being mentored in the craft of landscape painting. One key element in Church's artistic practice was his frequent sketching trips to gather ideas for future paintings. He had adopted this practice from Thomas Cole, who regularly made extended sketching trips to wild mountainous regions, including New York's Adirondacks. It's quite likely that Church would have told McEntee about his and Cole's sketching trips. He may even have described and praised the sketches and paintings Cole made from his visit to the Indian Pass in the Adirondack High Peaks and to Long Lake in 1846. Church may have urged McEntee to make a sketching trip of his own.

The idea appealed to McEntee. He would certainly have been familiar with Cole's popular landscape paintings. He also would have read Cole's influential "Essay on American Scenery" (1836), where Cole declared, "The most distinctive and perhaps the most impressive, characteristic of American scenery is its wildness."[1] McEntee must have concluded he needed to take his own wilderness sketching trip to properly complete his artistic education.

A romantic fascination with seeking beauty in the wilderness had taken hold of American artists during the decades immediately preceding the Civil War. It was a time when industrialization was on the rise and untouched wilderness was rapidly disappearing. As nature fell to the axe, plow, and miner's pick and shovel, the old fear of everything wild was gradually being replaced by a growing appreciation of the unspoiled landscape as a place of solace, a refuge from an increasingly urban world.

For about four decades, from roughly 1850 until 1890, many American landscape painters produced works that featured wilderness scenes. These paintings are characterized by a realistic and detailed but also a somewhat romanticized portrayal of nature. By 1870, landscape artists who painted such scenes were being collectively referred to as the "Hudson River School."

It's clear from entries in McEntee's journal that he had fully embraced this romantic view of nature before the sketching trip. His journal entries contain effusive, often over-the-top expressions drawn

---

1. Thomas Cole, "Essay on American Scenery," *American Monthly Magazine* 1 (Jan. 1836): 5.

from his reading of romantic writers of his time. McEntee especially admired the romantic nature poetry of William Cullen Bryant. Later in his career, McEntee would create a series of illustrations for a publication of Bryant's long poem *Among the Trees*. In a letter to Bryant's daughter on the occasion of her father's death in 1878, McEntee wrote, "What little I have been enabled to accomplish in Art has been largely due to him. I have always loved to paint from his suggestive verse and I strongly feel that the years as they go by will strengthen and hallow in my soul the gentle influence which he early planted there."[2]

By 1850, it was becoming increasingly difficult to find wilderness areas untouched by the rapidly advancing forces of the Industrial Revolution. McEntee could have easily chosen the Catskill Mountains near his home for a sketching trip, but they seemed too easy, too civilized. He instead settled on a difficult extended journey across the central Adirondacks. One reason for this choice was probably the fact that Cole had recently sketched in the Adirondacks. McEntee later remarked, however, that the deciding factor was the descriptions of wild Adirondack scenes in Joel T. Headley's recent account of his trips to the central Adirondacks, titled *The Adirondack; Or, Life in the Woods* (1849). McEntee discussed the idea of making an Adirondack sketching trip with Joe Tubby, who wanted to go along. In late winter 1851, the two friends started to plan the trek.

Biographical Sketches of the Artists

Although neither Jervis McEntee nor Joseph Tubby would achieve the success and fame of Frederic E. Church and some of the other leading figures of the Hudson River School, they would continue to sketch and

2. Jervis McEntee to one of Bryant's daughters (either Julia Sands Bryant or Frances "Fanny" Bryant Goodwin, 1878 (sometime after June 12, 1878, the date of Bryant's death), quoted in "Jervis McEntee: Biography," Hirschl & Adler, n.d., https://www.hirschlandadler.com/galleries/jervis-mcentee. See also William Cullen Bryant, *Among the Trees*, illustrated with designs by Jervis McEntee, engraved by Harley (New York: Putnam, 1874).

paint for the rest of their lives. In many ways, McEntee and Tubby as they appear in this book are like most aspiring artists. They believed in their talent and yearned to have others recognize it.

Just as they hoped, their sketching trip to the Adirondacks propelled them onward to lives devoted to art. McEntee would go on to a distinguished full-time career as a landscape painter. Although Tubby could afford to paint only in his spare time, his landscapes attracted many admirers and buyers over his lifetime. The works of both McEntee and Tubby can be found today in many museum collections. Here are some of the basic facts of their lives.

Jervis McEntee

Jervis McEntee grew up in what we would now consider an upper-middle-class family. He attended a private secondary school. After he left school, he lived at home, and his family helped support him for a few years while he worked to establish himself as a landscape painter. During the sketching trip, he presents himself in his journal as determined, optimistic, and easy-going, with a romantic, poetic nature.

His grandparents had emigrated from Ireland to rural Westernville, Oneida County, a short distance north of Rome, New York, in the late eighteenth century. His father, James S. McEntee, was born on the family farm in 1800. James's first job off the farm was as an axe man on a surveying team for the Erie Canal. In 1825, he married Mary Swan, a woman from his hometown. They immediately relocated to Kingston, New York, where James had obtained work as an engineer to help with the building of the Delaware & Hudson (D&H) Canal. Mary McEntee died unexpectedly in February 1826. In 1827, James became the resident engineer for the Rondout end of the D&H Canal. In late July 1827, he married Sarah Jane Goetchius of New Paltz, New York. Jervis was their first child, born on July 14, 1828. He was named after his father's mentor, John B. Jervis, an engineer from Rome, New York, who was James's supervisor on both the Erie and D&H Canals.

Jervis grew up in a busy hotel called the Mansion House that his family managed near Rondout Creek in the new and rapidly growing village. McEntee started to paint at an early age. His parents encouraged his interest by allowing him to set up a studio in their home. They also sent him and his brothers and sisters upstate to the Clinton Liberal Institute, a Universalist school in Clinton, New York, near Utica. During his school years from 1844 to 1846, the young Jervis kept a daily journal. In the opinion of the local historian Lowell Thing in Kingston, his school journal "suggests a playful and self-confident young man with a special interest in writing, languages (Latin and French), and politics, but no evidence of any formal art training."[3] In November 1846, he and his sister became ill and returned home. After he recovered, he decided not to return to school.

Back in Rondout, McEntee lived at home and seems to have worked in the village while continuing to paint in his spare time. He noted in his school journal for 1845–46 that his father had a summer job waiting for him in which he would help build an island dock in the Rondout Creek for the canal company. We know that he was already producing accomplished finished landscape paintings during 1847–49 because in 1850 he sold four paintings to the American Art-Union in New York City. In 1849, he convinced Frederic Edwin Church to give him some painting instruction, and so during the winter of 1850–51 he lived in a studio in the Art-Union Building and studied with Church.

In the fall of 1851, following the Adirondack sketching trip, McEntee returned home, and from 1852 until 1855 he worked in his uncle's flour-and-feed business while continuing to paint part-time. In 1853, he was able to build an art studio adjacent to his parent's home. The spacious studio was designed by the architect Calvert Vaux, who would later help design Frederic Church's nearby home, Olana. Three years after the Adirondack sketching trip, in 1854, Jervis married Anna Gertrude Sawyer, and they expanded the Rondout art studio into their home. The next year, 1855, McEntee took out an ad in his

---

3. Lowell Thing, curator, *Jervis McEntee: Kingston's Artist of the Hudson River School*, catalog, exhibition May 1–Oct. 15, 2015 (Kingston, NY: Friends of Historic Kingston, 2015), 7.

local newspaper to officially announce that he was now a professional landscape painter with his own studio.

When he learned in 1857 that a number of other Hudson River School painters were planning to live and work together in a purpose-built studio building on West Tenth Street in New York City, he and Gertrude rented a studio there. For the remainder of their lives, the McEntees lived at the Tenth Street Studio Building during the winter and at their Rondout home during the warmer months. Jervis was elected an associate of the American Academy of Design in 1860 and was elevated to academician in 1861.

For the rest of his life, McEntee made a living as a professional painter, although he would sometimes complain that his work was not selling well. Among his peers and critics, he enjoyed a reputation as a painter whose best work was philosophical and thoughtful. In 1868, he took a year-long tour of Europe with Gertrude, traveling and sketching. Gertrude died unexpectedly in 1878, when she was just forty-four. Although devastated by his loss, Jervis continued painting and traveling. During the 1880s, he took trips to Nevada, Wyoming, and other western states; he also took a trip to Mexico as a companion to his good friend Frederic Church. In 1890, he grew ill, most likely from kidney disease, and died on January 16, 1891. He was buried next to his beloved Gertrude in Montrepose Cemetery in Rondout (now Kingston). Writing in the *1892 Century Association Yearbook*, Harry E. Howland remarked of his friend, "Jervis McEntee held a high position, and was widely known and appreciated. There was a tender and melancholy sentiment in his work which made it exceedingly popular with the public, and his genial and unassuming nature endeared him to a host of friends."[4]

In addition to his large number of paintings, McEntee created an enduring legacy with his later journals. In nearly 4,500 detailed journal entries, now in the Archives of American Art at the Smithsonian

4. Harry E. Howland, "Report of the Board of Management," in *1892 Century Association Yearbook* (New York: Century Association, 1892), 23–24.

Institution, he provides a vivid, accurate impression of the life of a New York artist of the 1872–90 period. His journals preserve an intimate account of Hudson River School artists, their day-to-day life, gossip, and personal reflections. They also reveal the economics of the art world, including the prices of artworks, patterns of collecting and patronage, and the artists' dependence on personal contacts through clubs, social gatherings, and influential friends. His journals also cover his own artistic successes and trials, including his financial difficulties as the Hudson River School's popularity declined in the face of impressionism, a movement he despised.

Joseph Tubby

Joseph Tubby was born on August 25, 1821, in Tottenham, England. His parents, John Tubby and Mary Green, were Quakers. The family immigrated to New York in 1832 when Joe was eleven years old. His father established himself as a building contractor in the rapidly developing village of Rondout at the eastern terminus of the D&H Canal, which opened in 1828. Because of its commercial activity, Rondout quickly grew from 1,500 residents in 1840 to 6,000 residents in 1855, which made for very good business for a contractor.[5]

There is no evidence that Joe Tubby had any formal education beyond what was offered in the local common school. As a young man, Joe befriended Jervis McEntee and his cousin Julia McEntee (Dillon after she married), both of whom lived in Rondout and shared his interest in art. Like Jervis McEntee, Tubby was strongly influenced by the current interest in painting the natural landscape. He was mostly self-taught, but he also picked up tips on technique from his two artist friends. In his free time, he went on long walks throughout the Rondout area, making sketches of the scenery in his notebook.

During his teens and twenties, he probably worked for his father. He learned house painting and wallpapering. He also worked as a sign

5. Sanford A. Levy, curator, Joseph Tubby, 1861–1896, artist, Rondout, New York, catalog, exhibition May–Oct. 2008 (Kingston, NY: Friends of Historic Kingston, 2008), 6.

painter. He eventually specialized in the decorative painting popular at the time, trompe l'oeil. Many of his interior painting jobs involved transforming common wooden fittings so that they would appear to be marble or rare hardwoods. At the time of the Adirondack sketching trip in 1851, Tubby was twenty-nine years old. In "The Lakes of the Wilderness," McEntee describes him as a "plain man" and sums up Tubby's attitude toward life with a quote from Cicero, "esse quam videri" (to be rather than seem).[6] Judging from the way McEntee portrayed Tubby in the journal, Joe was a matter-of-fact, hard worker who took the difficulties and inconveniences of the sketching trip in stride without complaint.

Tubby's earliest known finished landscape painting dates to 1850. As noted in a letter to his family sent during the 1851 sketching trip (see letter 13), he was pleased to find out that while away on the sketching trip he had sold one of his finished paintings. In 1852, two of his landscape paintings based on sketches made in the Adirondacks were selected for the prestigious annual exhibit of the National Academy of Design.

In 1858, Tubby married Ella Hopkins, daughter of the minister of Wurts Street Baptist Church in Rondout. They had six children. After his marriage, he became more deeply involved in his father's contracting business. The success of that business allowed him the financial freedom to pursue his love of landscape painting on a part-time basis.

Tubby remained friends with Jervis McEntee and Julia McEntee Dillon for the rest of his life. In 1881 and 1882, he consulted them about his plan to discontinue his contracting business to concentrate on his art full-time. McEntee wrote in his diary that he tried to discourage his friend from this course because of the poor market for their style of landscape paintings.[7]

6. Jervis McEntee (no byline), "The Lakes of the Wilderness," *Great Republic Monthly*, Apr. 1, 1859, 336.

7. Jervis McEntee, journal, Nov. 30, 1881, and Jan. 3, 1882, Jervis McEntee Papers.

Tubby lived with his youngest daughter, Gertrude, in Montclair, New Jersey, during the last ten years of his life. He died in 1896 following a long illness and was buried near his two artist friends in the Montrepose Cemetery.

Organization of the Book

I have divided the sketching trip across the Adirondacks into three parts based on the two artists' extended stays at three base camps.

Part one, "Afloat on the Beaver River," takes them from their homes in Rondout to the village of Lowville on the western edge of the Adirondack wilderness and then describes their journey up the Beaver River to a guide's camp on the shore of Smith's Lake, later renamed "Lake Lila." They started out full of naive enthusiasm. They were so anxious to experience the thrill of hunting that they shot at birds and animals they had no intention of using as food. Even when faced with unexpected obstacles, McEntee's early journal entries are full of passages of discovery and amazement.

By the time they reached Smith's Lake, the artists had settled into a productive routine, sketching for part of the day, exploring and fishing the rest of the day. Their guide, Asa Puffer, hunted deer and prepared all the meals. McEntee bragged in the journal about how well they had adapted to the outdoor life even though some of their acquaintances had openly expressed doubts that they would last long in the wilderness. Things went well until June 24, when Puffer left camp to return to Lowville to acquire fresh supplies.

Alone in camp, McEntee and Tubby initially relished the solitude. It was not long, however, until their difficulties began to mount. Their food supply was low, and they caught few fish. They had trouble cooking for themselves; then both got quite sick. They hung around camp, feeling sorry for themselves. The insects were troublesome, and the weather provided them with thunderstorms on most days. All they could think about was how much they wanted Puffer to return. Needless to say, they were overjoyed when he showed up with fresh supplies, letters, and newspapers on July 2, the twenty-first day since they had departed from Lowville.

Part two covers their activities at Raquette Lake (which McEntee and Tubby refer to as "Racket Lake" or "Rackett Lake"), where the artists occupied the Constable family open camp on a scenic point on the lake for about two weeks. McEntee recorded that he wrote eleven letters during the first few days at Raquette Lake. They needed to hurry to finish their letters so Puffer could take them to the post office in Lowville when he returned there again for supplies on July 11. This time Puffer was absent for nine days because he needed a few days to bring in hay at his farm. When he returned to Raquette Lake on July 20, he brought along Joe Tubby's younger brother, Josiah, who remained with them for the rest of the trip. Puffer's absence did not greatly trouble the artists this time because in the weeklong interval between his absences Puffer had taught them some basic cooking and fishing skills.

During the Raquette Lake part of the trip, they met the famous Native American guides Lewis Elijah Benedict and Mitchel Sabattis. McEntee was quite taken with them. He reportedly made sketches of each of the men, but those portraits are now lost. McEntee proudly noted that Benedict allowed him to paddle his handmade birch-bark canoe and that he managed not to capsize it. McEntee also met and carefully described the two original white settlers of Raquette Lake, William Wood and Mathew Beach.

With each passing day, the artists became more confident in their artistic abilities. They sketched every day at Raquette Lake until they had completed sketches of every scene they thought worth their attention. McEntee's exquisite sketch of Wood's cabin, a copy of which follows this introduction, shows how well he had absorbed the atmosphere of the place. Their skill in woodcraft also improved markedly, illustrated by their easy paddle to Blue Mountain Lake, their climb up Blue Mountain in the rain, and their overland trek to Long Lake carrying their camping equipment.

At Long Lake, they took lodgings at William Austin's farm for five days. Their artistic goal, probably inspired by Cole's writing, was to make sketches of a dramatic waterfall scene in the area. They inspected two nearby falls and settled on the large falls of the Raquette

River near where it empties into Long Lake, now known as Buttermilk Falls. The wood engraving of the falls made from McEntee's sketch is attached to letter 22 in part two (figure 2.6). The scene looks nearly identical today.

The journey reaches its climax in part three, "High Peaks." McEntee and Tubby had two remaining goals: sketching the Indian Pass and climbing Mount Marcy, the highest peak in New York. Their desire to visit the Indian Pass was inspired by the well-known painting of it done by Charles Cromwell Ingham in 1837. In fact, they were so anxious to view it that they hiked there as soon as they arrived at the Upper Adirondac Iron Works, without waiting for their sketching and camping equipment to arrive.

The day after McEntee and Tubby finished their sketches of the Indian Pass, they set out to climb Mount Marcy. It took them two days to hike to the top. During the hike, McEntee sprained his knee when he slipped on a rock crossing a stream. Despite this injury, he continued the climb. They spent the night in a lean-to near the tree line and finally reached the summit early the next morning. They admired the panorama that stretched to the horizon in all directions, but before they could begin to sketch, clouds rolled in and obscured their view. They waited in vain for five hours for the clouds to part, then temporarily lost the trail as they descended.

The journal ends with McEntee still in camp at Henderson Lake waiting for his knee to heal. Joe Tubby and his brother had already left for home on their own. There was an emotional parting that illustrates how close the two artists had become. They would remain friends for the rest of their lives. Together they had endured much and learned much. Both were now more certain than ever that they were meant to be landscape painters and that they had the will and the skill needed to succeed in that profession.

Each of the three parts comes with an annotated map that traces the route and indicates the probable location of each of the camps where the artists stayed. An index map roughly showing the whole journey appears as figure M.0 here. These maps were created especially for this book by the talented cartographer Joseph W. Stoll.

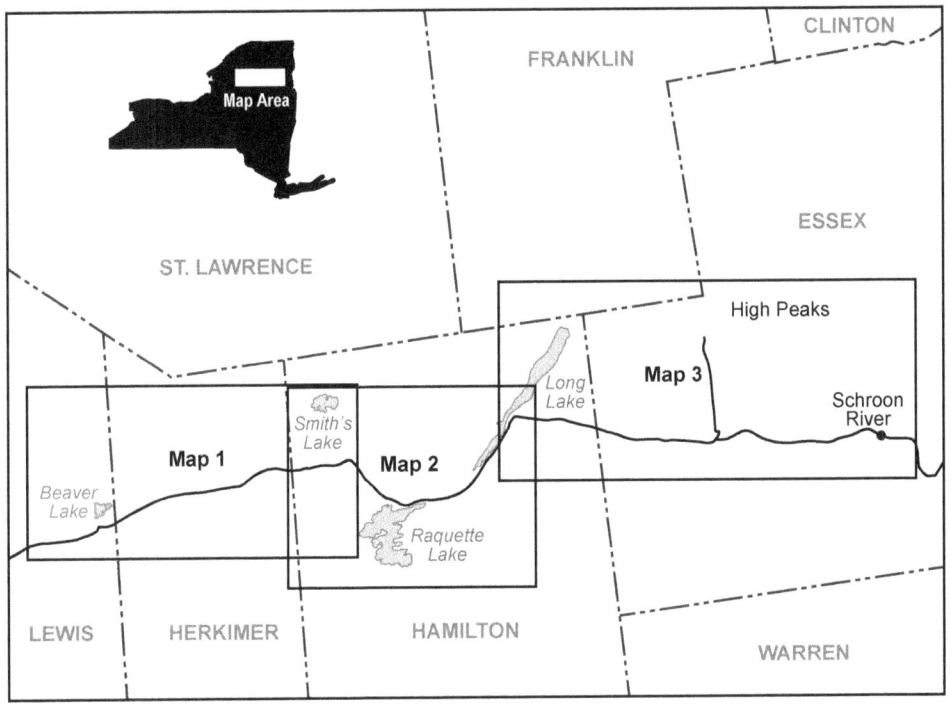

M.o. Index map of the entire trip. Joseph W. Stoll, Syracuse University Cartographic Laboratory.

The Source Materials

The story of the wilderness sketching trip told in this book is drawn primarily from the daily journal of Jervis McEntee. By this time in his life, McEntee was already dedicated to regularly keeping a journal. There is some evidence that he may have intended to later write about his experiences, but the journal itself was not written to tell the story of the sketching trip. It is simply a detailed record of events and impressions, including both the high points and the challenges.

Examination of McEntee's handwritten journal at the research library of The Adirondack Experience convinced me that it is most likely an edited copy of the actual daily journal McEntee kept during the trip. The copy is written out carefully in a bound ledger book, the last pages of which include what seem to be records of sales from his uncle's flour-and-feed store. There are no signs of wear on the book, as would be expected had it been carried along on the trip. A rough sketch of Puffer, their guide, cooking a trout, appears on the flyleaf. The writing is careful and uniform. Judging this copy from other examples of McEntee's handwriting in the Archives of American Art, we can conclude that McEntee himself transcribed it.

Two descriptive newspaper articles written by McEntee during the trip provide some additional details that complement the trip journal. An article about the early part of the trip appeared in his hometown weekly, the *Rondout Courier*, on July 18, 1851, titled "Rambles in the Adirondacks." A much longer piece titled "Camp Church, Ragged Lake, July 24, 1851" was published in two installments in the *Lowville Northern Journal* on August 20 and August 27, 1851. McEntee does not seem to have sent any articles about the latter part of the trip to any publication. Interestingly, he was not explicitly identified as the author of these newspaper articles. They are simply signed with his initials, "J. M."

Eight years after the trip, McEntee wrote a lengthy illustrated magazine article titled "The Lakes of the Wilderness," which appeared in the *Great Republic Monthly* on April 1, 1859. For some unknown reason, he chose to have the article published anonymously. McEntee also chose to use pseudonyms for himself and Tubby. He fictionalized parts of the narrative to include dialogue, poetry, and even song lyrics. And he omitted a great many of the interesting details of the trip. The magazine article does not always closely match the journal entries and sometimes diverges significantly. For this reason, when the accounts diverge, I consider the information in McEntee's journal and the newspaper articles to be more accurate.

It is somewhat ironic that it was this anonymous magazine article that led to the discovery and preservation of McEntee's trip journal and the other McEntee and Tubby Papers now in the Archives of American Art. The discovery of all this material in the mid-twentieth century was due to the efforts of Warder H. Cadbury, professor of philosophy at the State University of New York, Albany, who was then also a research associate for the Adirondack Museum (now renamed The Adirondack

Experience) in Blue Mountain Lake. While conducting research on a different project, Cadbury chanced upon a reference to "The Lakes of the Wilderness." By means of a series of educated guesses, he eventually concluded that McEntee was the author of the article.

This led him to contact the still-living descendants of both McEntee and Tubby. He discovered that Joseph Tubby's youngest daughter, Gertrude, possessed a trove of her father's papers. Among those papers was the handwritten McEntee trip journal of 1851. Relatives of McEntee possessed other documents, including McEntee's later journals. In 1964, at Cadbury's urging, Gertrude Tubby donated the McEntee journal along with her father's surviving memorabilia to the Archives of American Art, then housed at the Detroit Institute of Arts. In 1967, Cadbury arranged for the handwritten McEntee trip journal to be transferred to the Adirondack Museum, where it sits today, along with a typescript of it, probably created by Cadbury.[8]

The Illustrations

McEntee's journal mentions the many sketches he and Tubby made during the trip. After all, sketching the wilderness was their primary purpose. The journal especially highlights the sketches that they spent days creating, including those of the outlet of Smith's Lake, of Raquette Falls (now called Buttermilk Falls), and of the Indian Pass in the High Peaks. Unfortunately, these works and almost all of the other sketches McEntee and Tubby made on the trip have not survived. Fortunately, McEntee's original pencil sketch of Wood's cabin is in the collection of The Adirondack Experience. A copy of that sketch appears directly following this introduction. A complete review of all the known Adirondack sketches and paintings made by both McEntee and Tubby is provided in the concluding remarks at the end of this book.

McEntee's article "The Lakes of the Wilderness," published in the *Great Republic Monthly* in 1859, included eighteen wood engravings

---

8. See Warder H. Cadbury, "The Adirondack Bookshelf," *The Adirondac*, Mar.– Apr. 1964, 28–29.

created by the New York City firm of Loomis-Annin based on Mc-Entee's sketches. McEntee's initials, "JME," appear on some of the illustrations. Most of these engravings appear to be closely based on sketches he made during the trip, although a few were clearly created especially for the magazine article. Seventeen of the eighteen engravings from "The Lakes" are reproduced in this book. Only a small, undistinguished engraving titled "Blue Mountain" has not been included.

Many of these same engravings later appeared without attribution in a book about Lake George by B. F. DeCosta.[9] The captions were altered, and some identifying information was removed, but they are clearly the same images. How they came to be used in DeCosta's book is unknown.

9. B. F. DeCosta, *Lake George: Its Scenes and Characteristics, with Glimpses of the Olden Times. To Which Is Added Some Account of Ticonderoga, with a Description of the Route to Schroon Lake and the Adirondacks. With . . . Notes on Lake Champlain* (New York: A. D. F. Randolph, 1868).

o.1. Jervis McEntee, *The Lakes of the Wilderness*, wood engraving by Loomis-Annin from sketch by Jervis McEntee. In Jervis McEntee, "The Lakes of the Wilderness," *Great Republic Monthly*, Apr. 1, 1859, 335. Courtesy of the American Antiquarian Society, Worcester, MA.

0.2. Jervis McEntee, *Wood's Cabin at Rackett Lake*, pencil sketch, created July 18, 1851. Courtesy of The Adirondack Experience, The Museum on Blue Mountain Lake, Blue Mountain Lake, NY.

Sketching the Adirondacks

Part One | Afloat on the Beaver River

Rondout, New York, to Lowville, New York, to Smith's Lake, Headwaters of the Beaver River

June 12: By wagon and on foot by road from Lowville to Number Four, then on the Carthage–to–Lake Champlain wilderness road to O'Kane's shanty at Stillwater—29 miles

June 13: By boat on Beaver River to the Rock Shanty at Loon Lake— about 10 miles

June 14: By boat on Beaver River to Little Rapids—about 12 miles

June 15: By boat on Beaver River to site of the old bridge across Albany Lake—4 miles, including carry around the rapids of 0.75 mile

June 18: By boat on Beaver River to the Higby camp on Smith's Lake— 5 miles, including carry of 1.0 mile

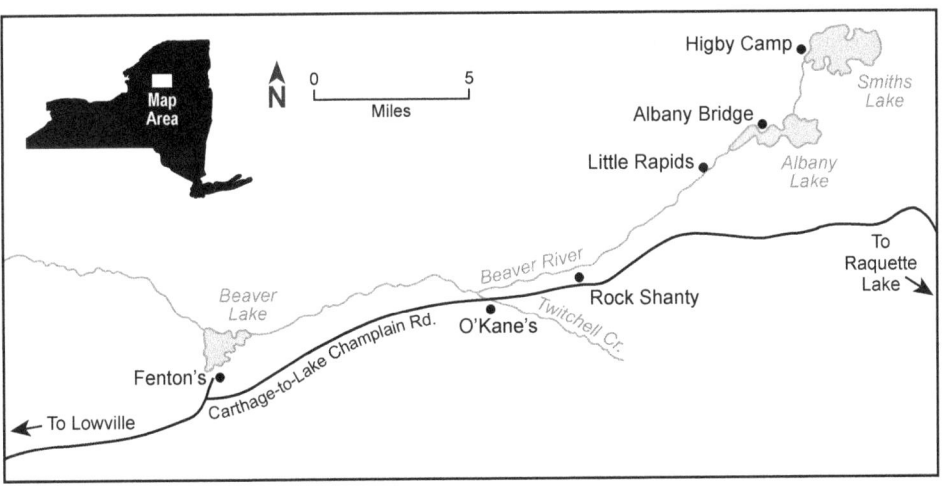

M.1. Map for part one. Joseph W. Stoll, Syracuse University Cartographic Laboratory.

Regarding the Feasibility of a Sketching Trip

To Mr. Jervis McEntee, the American
Art-Union Bldg., New York, New York
March 15, 1851

Dear Mr. McEntee,

This is in reply to your letter of February 28 addressed to Attorney Bostwick by whom I am employed. Mr. Bostwick passed your letter of inquiry to me because I am personally familiar with a portion of the great northern forest you propose to visit on a sketching trip this coming summer.

I caution you that such an extended wilderness journey would be feasible only if you are able to secure the services of an experienced and trustworthy local guide. A good guide will not only find the way but manage the baggage, cook the food and arrange for suitable sleeping quarters. I am acquainted with several honest local men who regularly work as guides for sportsmen, any one of which should be able to assist you for a reasonable sum.

You mention that you desire to visit certain locations described in the recent book by Headley. I have not read his book as yet, but if you have adequate time and funds, this can probably be arranged. I advise you to consider departing from my own village of Lowville on the western side of the wilderness. A woods road has recently been cut out that stretches from here the entire distance to Crown Point on Lake Champlain. By passing easterly along this road, you will undoubtedly be able to witness many if not all of the wild scenes you seek.

If this plan is agreeable to you, please advise if you would like me to make specific inquiries devised to acquire the services of a guide.

I am also quite willing to provide you with a detailed list of supplies you would need for an extended sketching trip in our wilderness.

Mr. Bostwick asks you to convey his greetings to your father. He made your father's acquaintance some years ago when your father was associated with the engineer John B. Jervis of Rome, a one-time client of Mr. Bostwick and who is, I believe, your namesake.

I remain, your obedient servant,
Nathaniel B. Sylvester
Office of Isaac W. Bostwick, Esq.
N. State St., Lowville, New York

Notes for Letter 1

This introductory letter is based primarily on McEntee's magazine article "The Lakes of the Wilderness," published in the *Great Republic Monthly* on April 1, 1859. McEntee's trip journal does not include any information on the planning of the trip. Information on the life of the Lowville attorneys Nathaniel Bartlett Sylvester and Isaac W. Bostwick is drawn from Franklin B. Hough's *History of Lewis County* (1883).[1]

McEntee and Tubby must have planned the sketching trip during the winter of 1850–51 while living in their shared art studio in New York City. At the beginning of "The Lakes of the Wilderness," McEntee explains that one of his primary reasons for choosing the central Adirondacks for the trip was his admiration of a popular book of the time, Joel T. Headley's *The Adirondack; Or, Life in the Woods* (1849).[2] Although captivated by Headley's descriptions of the wild scenery, McEntee was critical of this book because it provided so little in the way of helpful practical details. There is no evidence that either McEntee or Tubby had ever done much hunting or fishing or even camped out.

It makes sense, therefore, that they would have sought help in making their plans. This first letter is an imagined reply to McEntee's request for assistance. There is strong circumstantial evidence that it was Nathaniel Bartlett Sylvester who helped them plan the sketching trip. In "The Lakes," McEntee specifically says that he received help in deciding whether the sketching trip was feasible from "a friend" who lived on the edge of the Adirondack wilderness.[3] After arriving in Lowville, McEntee noted that "our friend" was the one who secured the services of Asa Puffer, their guide. On the first day of the trip, June 12, when McEntee realized he forgot some of his camping gear,

1. Franklin B. Hough, *History of Lewis County, New York, with Illustrations and Biographical Sketches of Some of Its Prominent Men and Pioneers* (Syracuse, NY: Mason, 1883).

2. Joel T. Headley, *The Adirondack; Or, Life in the Woods* (1849), reprinted with an introduction by Philip G. Terrie (Bovina Center, NY: Harbor Hill, 1982).

3. McEntee, "The Lakes of the Wilderness," 336.

he wrote a letter to "Sylvester" back in Lowville to retrieve it (letter 4). Finally, among the letters McEntee and Tubby received while camped at Smith's Lake was one for both of them from "Sylvester." The imagined contents of that letter from Sylvester are in letter 12 of June 28.

Nathaniel Bartlett Sylvester is best known today as the author of *Historical Sketches of Northern New York and the Adirondack Wilderness* (1877), one of the earliest credible histories of the Adirondack region.[4] He also authored numerous other books, including encyclopedic histories of Saratoga, Rensselaer, and Ulster Counties.

Sylvester moved to Lowville in 1847 or 1848 from his home farm in Denmark, Lewis County, New York. He studied law in the office of a local lawyer and was admitted to the bar in 1852. In 1854, he took over management of the Nicholas Low estate from Isaac W. Bostwick, who for many years managed not only the Low estate but the extensive land transactions of the Constable and Pierrepont families. There is no direct evidence that Sylvester studied law with Bostwick, but given Bostwick's prominence, he would have been an obvious choice. The fact that Sylvester took over management of the Low estate after Bostwick died adds weight to this surmise.

Isaac W. Bostwick was an early settler in the village of Lowville. He was born in New Haven, Connecticut, in 1776. He moved to Lowville very early in the nineteenth century to establish a law practice. He served as the land agent for Nicholas Low, for whom the village was named, a duty he assumed in 1806. By 1810, as a symbol of his importance in advancing the town's development, a street in the village was named for him. In 1821, he built a house on a large lot along North State Street. That house, known thereafter as "Bostwick Hall," was constructed of Talcottville limestone by the same stonemasons that had built Constable Hall a few years earlier. His law office was in his home, with access through a separate entrance. Bostwick Hall still stands, although its address is now 7636 Reed Terrace. Isaac W.

---

4. Nathaniel Bartlett Sylvester, *Historical Sketches of Northern New York and the Adirondack Wilderness* (1877; reprint, Peru, NY: Bloated Toe, 2014).

Bostwick died in Lowville at age eighty-one in 1857. There is no direct evidence that Bostwick knew McEntee's father or his father's mentor, John B. Jervis, but given their proximity and duties, that seems a reasonable possibility.[5]

5. Hough, *History of Lewis County, New York*, 91, 112, 313–15. Additional information on Sylvester and Bostwick was found through Ancestry.com.

Financing the Trip

To Mr. James S. McEntee, Clovertop, Rondout, New York
April 1, 1851

Dear Father,

I hope this letter finds you well. I expect you and mother are already busy with spring planting. I do hope the weather is cooperating with your always ambitious schedule.

I continue to spend part of every day, usually the morning hours, in the studio of Mr. Church. He has been very liberal with his time and is not much disturbed by my desire to witness his every brush stroke. His critiques of my own poor efforts at landscape painting have been kind and insightful. In the afternoon I return to my own studio and attempt such revisions as he suggests.

Every day I experience feelings of extreme gratitude at your generosity, without which I would not have had this opportunity. I hope to one day prove myself worthy of your faith in me and my fledgling talent as an artist.

I have read and reread the long letter I received from you yesterday. I well understand that the time has come for me to provide for my own way in the world. During my past months' sojourn in New York City I have sold only a small number of my paintings, hardly enough to pay my part of the studio rent. Although my fervor to make my name as an artist is unwavering, I therefore agree to your suggestion that I return home when my studies with Mr. Church conclude at the end of April.

I am grateful that you have arranged a situation for me at Uncle Charles's feed store. It will suit me well, I think, to live for a while at home. I do not, of course, expect to have to give up painting but will work diligently to earn enough at the store to pay my own way until such time as my art can financially support me.

While I understand your reluctance to furnish me any more funds to pursue my artistic ambitions, I beg you to consider one further remittance. This past January Mr. Church showed me a box of sketches he made during his annual trips about the New England states. As I admired them, he greatly praised their usefulness in obtaining ideas for later paintings. He advised me in the strongest terms to undertake a sketching trip of my own.

I discussed this with Joe Tubby. He expressed great enthusiasm for the idea and told me he dearly wished he could accompany me on the trip. About the same time I chanced upon a copy of Headley's book praising the striking scenes in the Adirondack wilderness. I immediately seized on the notion to make that my destination.

I had no understanding of how such a trip could best be arranged, so I sent an inquiry to Mr. Bostwick, a lawyer you once mentioned, who lives some distance north of Rome on the western edge of the northern wilderness. His associate, a man named Sylvester, replied with an offer of assistance in the endeavor. Based on my correspondence with Sylvester I am assured that a trip across the wilderness of two months duration could be managed for the total cost of about $100.

If you will advance me half of this sum as a loan and arrange with Uncle Charles to defer my employment until September, I would be eternally grateful.

Your obedient son,
Jervis

Notes for Letter 2

This second introductory letter proposes an answer to the question of how the sketching trip was financed. This question is not directly addressed in any of McEntee's writings. That Jervis McEntee's father provided funds for the trip is supported by an entry in McEntee's trip journal that he expected to receive a "remittance" from home.[1] At that point late in the sketching trip, McEntee's cash was running out, probably because of unexpected expenses. He must have written to his father requesting further financial assistance. His journal entry and the daily trips to the post office thereafter provide support for my assumption that McEntee was financially dependent on periodically receiving money from home.

James McEntee, Jervis's father, was modestly well-off, and he reasonably could have afforded to underwrite Jervis's share of the cost of the sketching trip. He was a successful practicing civil engineer with a distinguished reputation. In 1847 or 1848, he purchased a fifty-two-acre homestead called "Clovertop" located on the Weinbergh, a ridge above Rondout. Although James McEntee liked to think of it as a farm, and the 1850 census identified him as a farmer, he was still working full-time as a civil engineer.[2] In this letter, Jervis wisely participates in his father's aspirational image of the property as a farm. In reality, by 1851 James McEntee had made plans to turn a large portion of his land into a neighborhood and had even laid out a street lined with building lots. By the late 1850s, most of James McEntee's fifty-two acres had become a street for the homes of local brickmakers and other local

1. Jervis McEntee, "Journal of the 1851 Adirondack Sketching Trip," entry for Aug. 9, MS 67-019, Research Library, The Adirondack Experience, The Museum on Blue Mountain Lake, Blue Mountain Lake, NY. See also letter 23.

2. Census information on James McEntee comes from Ancestry.com, 1850 United States Federal Census (online database), 2009, https://www.ancestry.com/search/collections/8054/; original data from Seventh Census of the United States, 1850, residence data: 1850, home in 1850: Kingston, Ulster, NY, Records of the Bureau of the Census, Record Group 29, series M432, roll 607, p. 78a, National Archives, Washington, DC.

industrialists whose products were shipped down the Hudson to make possible the rise of New York City's buildings.[3]

Based on what is known about Jervis McEntee's life at the time of the sketching trip, it's also probable that he used his savings to cover some trip expenses. From the time he left school in 1846 to 1850 when he moved temporarily to New York City, he lived at home with his parents and likely worked at various jobs in Rondout. However, even though he must have had some of his own money, it seems unlikely that his savings from these jobs and the funds he derived from sale of a few paintings were adequate to fully fund the sketching trip. In addition, it makes sense that part of the cost of the trip was paid by Joseph Tubby, who had a job working for his father's construction business. Tubby or his family also likely provided funds to cover the expenses incurred by Josiah Tubby, Joe's younger brother, who accompanied the artists on the second half of the trip.

There is no direct evidence that Jervis's share of the trip expenses was either a loan or a gift from his father. It is a fact, however, that soon after he returned from the trip through the Adirondacks, he did indeed go to work as a clerk at a flour-and-feed store in Rondout. His uncle, Charles McEntee, owned just such a store, and it makes sense that McEntee worked there for the next several years while continuing to paint. In 1855, though, he publicly announced the existence of his landscape-painting business, and by 1857 he was painting full-time, with an art studio and showroom in New York City.

3. Lowell Thing, *The Street That Built a City: McEntee's Chestnut Street, Kingston, and the Rise of New York* (Delmar, NY: Black Dome Press, 2015), esp. "Jervis McEntee's Studio," 43–81.

The Trip to Lowville and Meeting Asa Puffer, Their Guide

To Mr. & Mrs. James S. McEntee, Clovertop, Rondout, New York
Sunday, June 8, 1851

Dear Mother, dear Father,

Joe Tubby and I safely arrived at the inn in the village of Lowville shortly after midnight last night. Thankfully our innkeeper had waited up for us and made us feel quite welcome. He lodged us in a clean, spacious room on the second floor and accommodated Rover, Joe's bull terrier, in the stable. The stagecoach ride from Rome over a very rough road was nearly unbearable. It took more than twelve hours, including several stops to change horses, exchange passengers, mail and goods and for us and our fellow travelers to refresh ourselves. I was glad the weather was fair and for my preferred seat behind the driver on top of the stage.

Asa Puffer, our guide, called on us at the inn this morning shortly after we finished breakfast. You will recall that Puffer is the very man recommended to us by our friend Nathaniel B. Sylvester, who lives in this village. By having Sylvester do the negotiating for us we were able to hire Puffer for the quite reasonable sum of $20 per month, especially given that many guides in these parts are known to charge $1 per day or even more.

I have to admit that on first impression Puffer falls far short of my idea of a woodsman. He is a local farmer about thirty-three years of age who claims years of experience in traversing the wilderness. He is a short, squat man with a broad chest and a somewhat dull, stolid countenance. Here is a quick sketch of him.

ASA PUFFER, THE GUIDE.

1.1. Jervis McEntee, *Asa Puffer, the Guide*, wood engraving by Loomis-Annin from sketch by Jervis McEntee. In Jervis McEntee, "The Lakes of the Wilderness," *Great Republic Monthly*, Apr. 1, 1859, 337. Courtesy of the American Antiquarian Society, Worcester, MA.

Sylvester thinks highly of Puffer and writes that he is quite well regarded in these parts. He is descended in an oblique direction from the famous Elder Puffer of the Methodist persuasion, who was widely admired for his honesty and hard work.

Because Sylvester vouchsafes for his honesty and skill, we will trust to his judgment and hope for the best. Puffer claims he just finished a few months cutting lumber and his rough hands certainly show the wear of spending the winter outdoors. He says he has been all over the north woods working as an axe man for a surveying party in Lower Canada and for Nelson Beach in laying out the Carthage to Lake Champlain Road. Since this is the road that we will follow for much of our sketching trip, his firsthand knowledge of the route should prove to be valuable.

It started to rain and blow hard this morning. Puffer advises that we should stay warm and dry in the village until the storm passes. In the meantime, he has taken an inventory of our supplies and given us a list of necessities we should acquire and knowledge of where we can easily obtain them about town. He says he has arranged for a neighbor of his to transport us and our baggage by wagon the thirty miles we have to travel by road before we can take to the water for the remainder of the way to Smith's Lake, where we plan to stay for two weeks. Puffer has also obtained use of a sturdy boat from a neighbor that is stored in the bushes along the Beaver River at Stillwater where we should easily find it.

I expect all will be in readiness for our departure for the north woods the day after tomorrow. I will endeavor to write again to relate our first day's adventures. Please share this letter and those that follow with our family and friends in Rondout.

Your obedient son,
Jervis

Notes for Letter 3

The facts in this letter and the sketch of Puffer are taken from McEntee's magazine article "The Lakes of the Wilderness." Unfortunately,
that article does not record how he and Tubby traveled from their
homes in Rondout to the Erie Canal. It is reasonable to assume that
they traveled up the Hudson River to Albany on one of the steamboats
or passenger sloops that regularly made that trip. When they reached
the east end of the Erie Canal, they would have transferred to a mule-
drawn packet boat to continue their journey west.

In "The Lakes," McEntee notes that he traveled as far as Rome,
New York, on a canal boat. He further claims without explanation that
his friend Tubby boarded the canal boat in Utica with his dog, a bull
terrier. In Rome, they caught a stagecoach north to Lowville. McEntee complains that the road was rough and that it was midnight by the
time they got to Lowville. Unfortunately, he does not name the inn
where they stayed, but he does cryptically refer to "Wood's" and the
"Dad House" as places they frequented in Lowville.

They remained in Lowville until June 12, waiting for the weather
to clear. They met with their guide, Asa Puffer, every day to discuss
the trip. They had arrived in Lowville with trunks filled with equipment, but much of it Puffer found to be unnecessary. Puffer winnowed
down the gear and took the unneeded items to his farm to be retrieved
after the trip. Puffer's experienced eye also noted that the artists had
failed to purchase quite a number of essentials. He gave them a list of
missing items and told them where they could acquire them locally.

Even with their gear limited to just the essentials, their baggage
was still extraordinarily heavy by modern standards. McEntee did not
provide a list of their equipment in any of his writings, but, based on
scattered references, it is possible to derive a fair idea of what they
took. Their frying pan, grill, and Dutch oven were cast iron. They
carried silverware, tin plates, and tin cups. Staple foods such as flour,
cornmeal, sugar, salt pork, butter, black tea, and rice easily weighed
fifty pounds or more. They hauled along a homemade canvas tent. Although they brought only one change of clothes, each of them needed

a wool sleeping blanket and a waterproof sheet to cover the evergreen boughs they often used as a mattress. Of course, each carried a gun, bullets, gunpowder, and a fishing rod.

Each of the artists also carried a wooden sketching box. Such boxes would have been eight-to-twelve inches wide, six inches deep, and two or three inches thick. They had a hinged top that when opened could serve as a sort of easel. Drawers held the necessary art supplies, including paper, small panels, some oil paint, dry pigment, a few brushes, a selection of pencils, and possibly even an assortment of colored pencils, chalk, or crayons. The boxes were secured with a lock, which we know because McEntee recorded that he twice lost the key to his sketching box. In addition, each artist had a folding stool and an umbrella.[1]

As should be obvious, it was impossible for them to carry all this gear for any distance. At a few points in the journey, they hired a horse and wagon, but much of the journey was by water, with the boat bearing the weight. When they were forced to carry their baggage, the distances were relatively short, and Puffer carried the lion's share of the load.

The fact that Puffer had worked as an axe man for Nelson Beach's surveying party in laying out the Carthage–to–Lake Champlain Road in 1841 is supported by Beach's diary in the archives of the Lewis County Historical Society.[2] McEntee would certainly have mentioned this in a letter to his father because his father got his start as an engineer by working as an axe man laying out the Erie Canal.

The cost of Puffer's services, $20 per month, is in line with the usual charge of guides of the time, which could be as high as $1 per day. In addition to the guide's pay, sporting tourists were expected

1. More information on typical sketching equipment used by Hudson River School artists in this period can be found in Eleanor Jones Harvey, *The Painted Sketch: American Impressions from Nature, 1830–1880* (Dallas: Dallas Museum of Art, Henry N. Abrams, 1998), 25–30.

2. Nelson Beach, "Journal of Proceedings Relative to the Carthage and Lake Champlain Road," 1841, transcription by Noel Sherry, Collection of the Lewis County Historical Society, Lowville, NY.

1.2. Jervis McEntee, *Hole in $100 Bill*, wood engraving by Loomis-Annin from sketch by Jervis McEntee. In McEntee, "The Lakes of the Wilderness," 350. Courtesy of the American Antiquarian Society, Worcester, MA.

to pay for food, ammunition, and incidentals, including boat rental, wagon rides, meals at hotels, and rooms rented. When adjusted for inflation, Puffer's monthly pay would be worth $665.96 in today's dollars. At the end of "Lakes," McEntee remarks that the total cost of the trip had put a sizable hole in a $100 bill, or $3,330 today. He emphasizes the cost with the sketch shown in figure 1.2.[3]

3. "Inflation Calculator," Official Inflation Data, Alioth Finance, Nov. 16, 2024, https://www.officialdata.org/us/inflation/1851?amount=20; McEntee, "The Lakes of the Wilderness," 350.

First Day, Trip to Number Four, the Forgotten Bag

Carried by hand to the Hon. Nathaniel B. Sylvester, Esq.
Thursday, June 12, 1851

My dear Sylvester,

I was much pleased to enjoy your hospitality yesterday. You have done us a great service by assisting with the planning of our sketching trip, so I was glad to have the opportunity of thanking you for your efforts in person.

Joe and I departed hastily from your village this morning, bound for Stillwater on the Beaver River. We left the inn in such an excited state that we neglected to collect all our baggage from the landlord. A carpetbag containing spare clothing, tobacco and such was overlooked. I would be much in your debt if you could retrieve this bag and arrange to send it to us with the party of men to be guided by Higbie, who, as you know, plans to join us this coming week.

As I write, we are having our dinner in the kitchen of your friend Orrin Fenton at his little red house overlooking Beaver Lake. Fenton's wife Lucy is, as you rightly advised, a very able cook. I doubt we will see such good a meal for a long time. As soon as we finish and our driver's horses have been fed and watered, we will set off again for O'Kane's at Stillwater, where we plan to spend the night tonight.

I especially want to thank you for your part in obtaining the services of Puffer as our guide. So far, he seems an apt companion. The cart and driver he arranged met us promptly this morning. Puffer himself joined us where the bridge crosses the Black River. Joe and I were amused by the fact that Puffer's entire outfit for a whole summer in the wilderness consists of only his well-used rifle and "whatever comforts he needs tied in a cotton handkerchief."

We are all in high spirits. As we walked along after the wagon, we amused ourselves by fooling with our newly acquired guns and waving to people at farms as we passed by. Tubby's dog scared up a rabbit, but we were too unprepared to shoot it. Afterwards we did shoot half a dozen pigeons. I plan to give Mrs. Fenton most of them and only keep two for tonight's supper.

Remember, we are holding open our invitation for you to join us for fishing at Smith's Lake but understand that your business may be too pressing for you to do so at this time. It would be pleasant to see you again and show you some of my new sketches of your favorite haunts along the Beaver.

With kind regards, your friend,
Jervis McEntee

Notes for Letter 4

This letter is based on the first entry in McEntee's trip journal. Mc-
Entee recorded that he and Tubby left the inn in Lowville at 8:00 a.m.
in a wagon drawn by a team of horses driven by a man identified only
as "our driver." They met Puffer a few miles along the way at Beach's
Bridge, where there has long been a bridge across the Black River.
McEntee claims they arrived at the Fenton house in the small settlement called "Number Four" about 10:00 a.m. This timing is unlikely,
to say the least. Number Four is eighteen miles from Lowville. Loaded
wagons usually made three to five miles an hour. A person on foot can
walk three to four miles an hour. Assuming the travelers rode part of
the way, the trip would have taken at least four and a half hours, meaning they would not have reached Number Four before 12:30 p.m. at
the earliest. Perhaps they left Lowville earlier than 8:00 a.m., in which
case they might have reached Fenton's before the noon hour, in keeping with the journal entry.

The two artists tried out their shotguns by killing half-a-dozen
pigeons as they walked along the Number Four Road. It's likely that
these birds were either mourning doves or passenger pigeons because
domestic pigeons were found primarily in towns and cities, and passenger pigeons were not yet extinct in North America.

In the pioneer village of Number Four, McEntee and Tubby
stopped for dinner at the Fenton homestead. *Dinner* in this era referred to the midday meal and *supper* to the evening meal. Orrin
and Lucy Weller Fenton were early settlers of Number Four, having arrived in 1826. As was the case with most nineteenth-century
sportsmen's hotels, the Fenton family got into the hotel business by
providing meals and renting rooms in their homestead to the occasional passersby. Fenton's remained a modest place during Orrin
and Lucy Fenton's tenure. They raised their five children at Number Four while eking out a wilderness subsistence by renting rooms,
guiding, hunting, fishing, and gardening. They reluctantly sold their

homestead in 1863 and moved to the village of Watson after residing at Number Four for nearly forty years.[1]

1. W. Hudson Stephens, *Historical Notes of the Settlement on No. 4, Brown's Tract, in Watson, Lewis County, N.Y. with Notices of the Early Settlers* (Utica, NY: Roberts, 1864), 11–14, 25–27.

Meeting the Hermit Jimmy O'Kane
at Stillwater

To Mr. & Mrs. James S. McEntee, Clovertop, Rondout, New York
Friday, June 13, 1851

Dear Mother, dear Father,

Our trip is off to a glorious start! We arrived here at Stillwater on the Beaver River at sunset yesterday after walking for nearly thirty miles behind the wagon loaded with our baggage. The road was so rough that riding was more tiresome than walking, 'tho I admit, I did ride the last few miles because my feet were sore from my ill-fitting boots.

The concerns expressed in my previous letter to you about the wisdom of hiring Puffer as our guide are proving to be unfounded. He is strong, quiet and wise in the ways of the forest. He shot a fine deer yesterday, then made us supper with some of it along with some salt pork, a boiled pigeon, crackers and black tea. There is no need for you to worry for our safety. I can assure you we are in the best of hands. With Puffer's able assistance our trip is bound to be nearly carefree.

Last night we stayed at the rude cabin of a man named Jimmy O'Kane at the place where the road meets the Beaver River above miles of rapids. O'Kane's shanty is at the edge of a tract of burned trees quite close by a shaky log bridge that spans a deep creek so those that dare cross can continue on the road to Racket Lake. The cabin is built of logs with a bark roof, one window and a door. There is a small cooking stove, a homemade table and chair, and in the corner a barrel of foul-smelling stuff O'Kane calls his emergency provisions. There is barely room for three men, much less five of us, to lie down. I was most fortunate to claim a spot furthest from O'Kane.

Sylvester had told us of O'Kane, but his description did not adequately prepare me for what we encountered. "O'Kane is tall, very tall, being six foot three inches, and although he stooped considerably, this was the first thing we remarked about him. He has long black hair and the unmistakable features of an Irishman and though we might have doubted from whence he came[,] these doubts were put to flight at the sound of his voice."

He lives alone with only a mongrel dog for company. His clothes are old, tattered and quite dirty. "Taking him altogether with his huge frame, his sunblossomed face, his old gray cravat and unctuous woolen shirt, he was decidedly an unpleasant-looking chap to sleep with in a log cabin."

I was unable to discover why he had come to this remote spot or where he was from. He says he has lived here for about six years. In answer to my questions about his reason for living as he does, he could give no coherent reply. "Presently he went to a corner of the cabin and returned with three or four old bags of straw, black with grease and dirt, that he threw down for our mattresses." After some further wandering conversation, "he wrapped himself in an old blue military overcoat and amid mutterings and growls he slid off into the quiet land."

I was tired to the bone, but I did not sleep well. I awoke in the cold dawn, fevered and unrefreshed, although a wash down at the lake made me feel much better. As soon as breakfast was done, we packed our baggage in a sturdy boat we rented from O'Kane. Since we will travel from here by water, our driver is already hitching up his team in preparation for return to the village. I will end here as I must pass this letter to the driver so he can carry it out to the post in Lowville. I will write again as soon as I'm able.

Your obedient son,
Jervis

Notes for Letter 5

McEntee, Tubby, and Puffer walked the eleven miles from Fenton's to Stillwater during the afternoon of the first day. From the very start of the trip, McEntee complained about his ill-fitting and poorly made boots. The poor condition of his boots forms a sort of subplot through the entire trip.

The bulk of this letter contains McEntee's observation of the hermit Jimmy O'Kane, drawn directly from the journal. His description of O'Kane and his cabin are consistent with those found in other first-person accounts. It is likely that McEntee had some advance knowledge of O'Kane courtesy of Sylvester, who personally visited O'Kane on several occasions during the 1850s.[1]

O'Kane was also known to the Constable family, who traveled along the Carthage–to–Lake Champlain Road several times during the 1850s on their way to Raquette Lake. John Constable described O'Kane as "a miserable specimen of humanity, who, according to his own account, has been living at this spot for the past seven years, in a wretched shanty, with no companion but a dog."[2]

A group including the editor of the *New York Daily Times*, Henry Jarvis Raymond, stopped for their midday meal at O'Kane's shanty in the summer of 1855. Raymond called the shanty "Jimmysville." He characterized it as a "small, low wrenched hut." He noted that O'Kane was tall, unshaven, and covered by dirty rags that had once been pants and jacket, as "savage, wrenched and repulsive [in] appearance as can be imagined."[3]

1. See Sylvester, *Historical Sketches of Northern New York and the Adirondack Wilderness*, 137–39.

2. Bob Racket [pseudonym of John Constable], "A Month at the Racket," *The Knickerbocker* (1856), reprinted in Edith Pilcher, *The Constables: First Family of the Adirondacks* (Utica, NY: North Country, 1992), 72.

3. Henry Jarvis Raymond, "A Week in the Wilderness," *New York Daily Times*, 1855, reprinted in Harold K. Hochschild, *Township #34: A History with Digressions of an Adirondack Township in Hamilton County in the State of New York* (New York: Published by the author, 1952), addendum to chap. 13, 170–75.

When Sylvester visited O'Kane in May 1857, he found him feeble and ill, noting, "It was the first day of the spring in which he had been able to crawl out to the bridge across the creek and set his poles for fishing."[4] O'Kane died the following January. He was buried at Stillwater, supposedly at his favorite spot on the high bank of Twitchell Creek. O'Kane's imaginative obituary appeared in the *Lowville Northern Journal* in January 1858.[5]

4. Sylvester, *Historical Sketches of Northern New York and the Adirondack Wilderness*, 138.

5. O'Kane's obituary is reprinted in Stephens, *Historical Notes of the Settlement on No. 4*, 23–24.

Trip up the Beaver River
and Impressions of Albany Lake

To Miss Julia McEntee, c/o Mr. Charles McEntee,
Rondout, New York
Sunday, June 15, 1851

Dear Cousin Julia,

I trust my parents have shared my prior letters with you. If so, you know that Joe and I reached the Beaver River at Stillwater three days ago. During the next two days we gradually ascended that twisting watercourse, traveling a leisurely ten miles or so each day, fishing and greatly enjoying ourselves. Last night we camped at the foot of some rapids that halted our further progress. We pitched our tent there for the first time. Our guide, Puffer, had a good laugh at us as we struggled with the canvas. Joe once lost his grip on the branch we were using for a ridgepole and was rewarded by a sharp knock on the head. Presently we got the tent up but I wonder if it is worth the trouble as there appear to be plentiful shanties along our route.

We planned to stay a day or two at the rapids to do some sketching but were encouraged to find a better spot by dense clouds of mosquitos and biting flies called punkies. Early this morning we decided to move to a better spot where Puffer said the flies might be more tolerable.

We ascended the rapids without much difficulty. Puffer had moved the boat above the "Little Rapids" last evening, so our day began with an easy one-mile row to reach the base of the "Long Rapids," being about a half mile in length. Joe and I took knapsacks of gear, our guns and rods around through the woods while Puffer pulled the boat, still partly filled with baggage, up through the rapids by a chain fastened to the front.

Above the rapids the river spreads out, forming a beautiful lake with many bays and inlets. As we rounded a point, we came to a narrows, where we found the ruins of the old Albany Road bridge. "It makes an interesting scene, standing as it does so far from civilization. The bridge is in a dilapidated condition, though not as much as I should imagine it to be in that length of time, nearly forty years having elapsed since it was constructed." All that is left are the crumbling piers and rotting heavy timbers that once supported a road. The bridge surface is completely gone, having been used for building shanties, for firewood and such.

"Standing as it does in such a wild and lonely spot, it impressed me forcibly at first sight. I thought of the time when these woods rang to the sound of the axe, and the hum of industry churned these deep solitudes; horses, the shouts of the artisans swelled across the lake affrighting the deer and the screaming fish hawk from their heretofore uninvaded abodes. But they who built it have passed away, and the forest is quiet again, and its depths in all probability will never again echo to the tread of an army."

We landed near the bridge, and following the faint trace of the road we found a bark shanty on a small rise facing the lake. Because we were out of meat and our day's fishing had been unsuccessful, as soon as we moved the necessities to the shanty Puffer went out hunting for deer. Joe and I both stayed behind to sketch, to write letters and make notes in our journals. As evening approached, Puffer returned with a buck he had shot and prepared some of it for our supper.

Enclosed is the sketch I made this afternoon of the old bridge. I hope it conveys the mood of this place better than my words can do. As I sat on a boulder by the shore, Joe sketching beside me, we both remarked on how much we missed your company and critical eye for detail. We shall surely have much to discuss after you see our new sketches on our return. I look forward to the three of us going a-sketching together again this fall.

RUINS OF BRIDGE, ALBANY LAKE.

1.3. Jervis McEntee, *Ruins of Bridge, Albany Lake*, wood engraving by Loomis-Annin from sketch by Jervis McEntee. In McEntee, "The Lakes of the Wilderness," 340. Courtesy of the American Antiquarian Society, Worcester, MA.

Please give my greetings to your father and thank him for his part in allowing me time for this adventure. I shall send this letter out with Puffer when he returns to town for supplies late next week. I would be most happy to hear your news in reply. Puffer can convey your letter to me on his return from a subsequent trip to town.

Sincerely,

Jervis

Notes for Letter 6

At the heart of this letter are a description and drawing of the remains of a bridge over the Beaver River, probably built in 1814 for a wilderness road intended to connect the city of Albany with the St. Lawrence River Valley. The Albany Road, as it was called, wound its way north from older established roads out of the Mohawk Valley, passed near present-day Speculator, New York, and crossed the Beaver River over a narrow section of Albany (now Nehasane) Lake. From there the road continued north, crossed the Oswegatchie River, then connected to the St. Lawrence Turnpike about ten miles south of the village of Russell.

The Albany Road was authorized by the New York Legislature on June 19, 1812, and completed to the vicinity of Russell in 1815. Despite what the state legislature may have believed when it made this authorization, there was very little need for the road. Because most of it was never maintained, the forest quickly returned, and the road became impassable.

McEntee appears to have heard that the Albany Road was a military road connected in some vague way to the War of 1812. He probably got this information from Puffer, but there is no evidence to support this story. The Albany Road was not completed until three years after the end of that war, and there are no accounts of it ever being used by troops. The St. Lawrence Turnpike was used to move supplies and troops. Since the Albany Road eventually connected to the St. Lawrence Turnpike, it may have obtained its military connotation by loose association.[1]

This letter is addressed to Jervis's cousin Julia McEntee, the daughter of his father's younger brother, Charles McEntee, who owned a flour-and-feed store in Rondout. Julia was born in 1834, so at the time of the trip she would have been seventeen and still living with her parents. Like Jervis, she was educated at the Clinton Liberal Institute. I

---

1. Edward I. Pitts, *Beaver River Country: An Adirondack History* (Syracuse, NY: Syracuse Univ. Press, 2022), 46–47.

imagine that Jervis wrote to her when he wanted to express his artistic reactions to special scenes he encountered.

Julia had become deeply interested in art during her studies at the Clinton Liberal Institute. Sometime during her teen years, her cousin Jervis introduced her to his artistically inclined friend Joseph Tubby, and the three often went sketching together in the Hudson Valley. The three artists remained friends all their lives. In later years, they would occasionally gather at Jervis's studio in New York City to compare paintings and discuss the art world of the time.

In 1866, Julia married John Dillon, owner of a successful Rondout iron foundry. After her husband's untimely death in 1873, she became a partner in the McEntee and Dillon Rondout Foundry and Machine Shop. She remained an active partner in the business for the rest of her life, which gave her the financial freedom to pursue her art career.

Still-life paintings of roses, chrysanthemums, and other flowers became her specialty. Her early studies in Paris in 1872 and time spent working in her cousin Jervis's studio led to an exhibition at the National Academy of Design in 1876. After that success, she exhibited at the World's Columbian Exhibition in Chicago, the Art Institute of Chicago, the Brooklyn Art Association, the Pennsylvania Academy of the Fine Arts in Philadelphia, and the Boston Art Club.[2]

As McEntee reports in this letter, he and Tubby reached Albany Lake on the third day after leaving O'Kane's at Stillwater. They spent the first night after leaving O'Kane's at a trapper's cabin known as the Rock Shanty about ten miles upstream from Stillwater. The second night was in a tent at the foot of the Little Rapids. Their pace was leisurely. They spent time fishing, loafing, and pulling the boat over beaver dams and logs jammed into narrow spots in the river.

They did no sketching during the two days on Beaver River. McEntee would later explain in a letter to the *Lowville Northern Journal*, "We were two days ascending the stream which is a decidedly

2. Charles Glasner and Sanford A. Levy, curators, *Julia McEntee Dillon: A Retrospective*, catalog, exhibition May–Oct. 2005 (Kingston, NY: Friends of Historic Kingston, 2005).

uninteresting one passing with a crooked and sluggish current through low alder meadows and affording not a single view worth the trouble of sketching."[3] The first sketch McEntee mentions in his journal is of the derelict Albany Bridge, reproduced as figure 1.3 here.

3. Jervis McEntee, "'Camp Church,' Ragged Lake, July 24, 1851," *Lowville Northern Journal*, Aug. 20 and 27, 1851, copy and typescript in the research library of The Adirondack Experience, The Museum on Blue Mountain Lake.

The Beauty of the Wilderness

To Miss Anna Gertrude Sawyer, c/o Dr. Thomas Jefferson Sawyer, principal, the Clinton Liberal Institute, Clinton, New York Monday, June 16, 1851

Dear Gertrude,

In my last letter to you I told you how my father wanted me to return home and enter a trade. He has been very understanding about my devotion to art, but I cannot deny that I have called upon his generosity for longer than I should have done. He has arranged with my uncle Charles for me to work in the feed store to earn a little money while I decide what trade best suits me.

I know in my heart that the only "trade" I want to follow is landscape painting. My time with Mr. Church this past winter convinced me of that. I suspect father knows as much, so when I begged him to let me have this summer for a sketching trip, he agreed. In turn I agreed to move back home in Rondout and start work at Uncle Charles's store in September.

I write you from our camp at a place called Albany Lake far into the Adirondack wilderness along the twisting Beaver River. I am here with my good friend Joseph Tubby, who also desires a profession as an artist. We acquired the services of a local man, a farmer called Puffer, to serve as our guide and protector—and serve us he does with much skill but very little conversation.

Knowing as I do how much you enjoy singing, I could not help but write you about Puffer's singing. We were rowing merrily along yesterday when a breeze came up. Joe opened his umbrella, and to all our delight it served in its way as a sail propelling our boat forward with ease. Suddenly "Puffer took his pipe from his mouth and broke forth in a peculiar air, the distinguishing characteristics of which were a complete unlikeliness to anything that has ever been sung or spoken, and a reckless and defiant disregard for any sound that might suggest melody." Joe and I tried not to laugh, then joined in the chorus as best we could.

> "I'm happy when I'm with her,
> And I'm happy when alone,
> And I'm happy when I'm hunting
> With my dog and my gun."

Last night Puffer and I went out with the boat to hunt deer by moonlight. "Presently I grew very cold and the fog . . . rose from the water as to prevent us almost entirely from shooting and the full moon coming up from which the dead branches of the balsams lit up our homeward path. Occasionally a duck rose from the water almost directly under our bow, the doleful hoot of the owl came over the water from the shore, and across the gleaming lake from some far bay shadowy with balsam and tamrock; the scream of the loon rang wild in the stillness of the night. How strange, how melancholy, how perfectly fitting to the solitude of the midnight woods are the sounds that leap from their depths and echo their sounding aisles."

I could not be more sure that there is something here for me that will make my art come alive. My fondest hope is to capture what I see and feel with my pencil and paint.

Your friend,

Jervis

Notes for Letter 7

This lighthearted letter captures the spirit of the trip so far. Both artists were having the time of their lives and were quite pleased with themselves. They had adopted a respectful attitude toward Puffer but were still amused by his backwoods manners. The descriptive passages in this letter are taken from McEntee's journal; however, Puffer's song appears only in "The Lakes."

The letter is addressed to a young woman Jervis probably first met when he attended the Clinton Liberal Institute. Anna Gertrude Sawyer, who preferred being called "Gertrude," was the eldest daughter of Caroline Fisher Sawyer and the school's principal, Dr. Thomas Jefferson Sawyer. Since Gertrude was born in 1834, at the time Jervis first met her she would have been only twelve years old and was seventeen at the time of the sketching trip in 1851, still living with her parents. There is no evidence that McEntee had a romantic relationship with Gertrude prior to the trip, but he must have been attracted to her because only three years after the trip, in 1854, they were married.

Gertrude was frequently praised for her social skills and her sunny disposition. In a later journal entry, Jervis recalled that at the time of their marriage he felt their love would be eternal.[1] Beginning in 1858, the couple rented a studio at the Tenth Street Studio Building in New York City. As the only married couple in the building, Jervis and Gertrude often hosted gatherings of the other artists who kept studios there.

Gertrude had a special talent for music. She played the piano and was an accomplished singer. She sang for the artists gathered at their studio and in a choir at a church on Fifth Avenue. She also sang sentimental favorites at McEntee family gatherings in Rondout. She once played the lead in a Kingston performance of "Esther," an oratorio by George Frideric Handel.

Gertrude Sawyer McEntee died unexpectedly in 1878 at the age of forty-four after only a week's illness. Jervis was devastated and never

1. Thing, *Jervis McEntee*, 22.

fully recovered from his grief. He visited the Montrepose Cemetery weekly whenever he was in Rondout and planted morning glories on her grave.[2]

In this letter, Jervis casually mentions that he and Puffer were out hunting deer from their boat at night. This once commonplace hunting method was called "jacklighting." Guides were well aware that deer commonly come to the water's edge after dark to drink. They also knew that shining a bright light in a deer's eyes would cause it to freeze for a few moments. Once a deer was located, the guide would hold up a special lantern called a "jacklight" that emitted a focused beam. The startled deer would usually prove to be an easy target for the amateur hunter in the boat. McEntee mentions Puffer using this method on several occasions. Many years later, jacklighting was outlawed in New York.[3]

2. Gertrude's biographical information is drawn primarily from Thing, *Jervis McEntee*, 22–24, and Thing, *The Street That Built a City*, 52. Some other facts are drawn from information on Ancestry.com.

3. See New York Environmental Conservation Law, Art. 11, Title 9, sec. 11-0901, subsection 4 (b)(2).

Meeting William Higby, a Model Adirondack Guide

To Miss Augusta McEntee, Clovertop, Rondout, New York
Tuesday, June 17, 1851

Dear Gussie,

I'm writing this as the sun fades on our camp overlooking Albany Lake. Here's a little sketch of me as I imagine I might look.

We sleep in a slanted-roof shanty called an open camp. It has two poles at the front made from stout tree branches that support a roof of woven saplings reaching diagonally to the ground. The roof is covered with sheets of bark to keep off the rain. For a mattress we lay fresh branches of evergreens on the ground inside. When topped with a blanket it is tolerably comfortable.

This morning Joe and I rowed out to a little island to make sketches and do some fishing. The wind came up suddenly as we prepared to land, which caused the boat to run hard onto the rocks, so now it leaks a little, but not so much as to be a bother. After we sketched, we fished for our dinner. I was lucky to catch twelve fine trout. Joe also caught a large one.

We worked on our sketches until dinnertime, then rowed back to camp. The wind was at our back this time, making the journey a quick one. Back in camp we prepared the fish by scraping off the scales then cutting them into fillets. Puffer, our guide, cooked the larger ones for our dinner, which we enjoyed with a few of his camp biscuits and some salt pork. He showed us how to drape the smaller fillets over a low fire to dry and smoke, so they can serve for our future breakfasts.

As we scaled the trout, I was acutely aware that the fine jackknife in my hand was a parting gift from you. I did not realize at the time

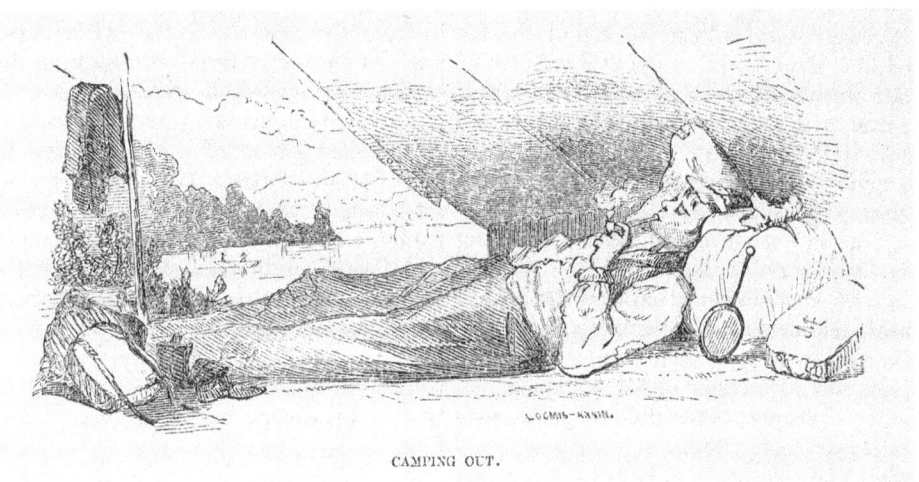

CAMPING OUT.

1.4. Jervis McEntee, *Camping Out*, wood engraving by Loomis-Annin from sketch by Jervis McEntee. In McEntee, "The Lakes of the Wilderness," 339. Courtesy of the American Antiquarian Society, Worcester, MA.

how invaluable a tool it would become. I use it daily for every possible task from sharpening my pencil to preparing meals. I thank you again a thousand times and determine to keep it forever in memory of your kindness and thoughtfulness.

I was writing in my journal about 3 o'clock this afternoon when Puffer, who was down by the shore, shot off his gun. Joe and I hurried down just in time to see a boat with three men aboard pull up to where Puffer stood waiting. It was the famous guide Higbie and two sportsmen in a lightweight boat designed and built by Higbie. Off in the distance down the lake we could just spy two more men in another of Higbie's boats making way towards us.

Presently the newcomers were settled in another open camp nearby, unfortunately one without our fine view. While Puffer busied himself making a venison supper for all of us, Higbie, a much more talkative fellow than Puffer, told us of his recent exploits guiding the Constable family to Racket Lake, where we would presently travel, then he showed us a way to arrange our blankets to stay warmer at night.

"Higbie pleases me much. He is a man of about fifty, stout, sedate, and yet kind and affectionate as a child. He comes up perfectly to my idea of a Jimmie Woodsman, and the more I see of him the better I am convinced of his kindness, and more, of his skill in all matters connected with the glorious wood life. In a little bag he carries innumerable little tools such as screws, screwdrivers, awls, etc., and he was not at all disconcerted on discovering he had left his candles and mold at Stillwater, for he had tallow with him and using a branch of alder he made two candles as fine ones as could have been made when men have better tools to work with."

We expect to depart here tomorrow bound for a camp Higbie built earlier this spring on Smith's Lake. I will write about our further adventures from there. Please share this letter with the family and write me to tell me your news.

Affectionately, your brother,

Jervis

Notes for Letter 8

I have addressed the various letters that describe McEntee's encounters with Adirondack guides to his younger sister, Augusta "Gussie" McEntee. She was born in 1833, so she would have been eighteen at the time of the trip. McEntee was quite interested in the guides he met. He devotes significant space in his journal to describing what he felt were their most unique characteristics. McEntee also often mentions in his journal how much he looked forward to letters from home. Puffer brought him bundles of letters at Smith's Lake and Raquette Lake. There was also a post office at the Upper Adirondac Iron Works. When camped at Smith's Lake in late June, Jervis reported he received a long letter from Gussie.

The first guide McEntee encountered other than Puffer was William Higby—not "Higbie," as McEntee spells it in his journal. William R. Higby was a neighbor and friend of Asa Puffer. He was born in May 1809. At the time of this trip, he would have been forty-two years old, not fifty, as McEntee surmised. In 1850, 1851, and 1855, Higby guided family camping trips to Raquette Lake for the wealthy Constable family. John Constable nicknamed him "Higby the Hunter." At the time of the Constable trip in 1850, Higby built the open camps on a point on Raquette Lake where McEntee and Tubby would stay in July 1851. He was one of the most respected early Beaver River guides. He left home briefly to serve in the Civil War, then returned to Lewis County and resumed guiding.[1]

Higby built the lightweight boats that he used for guiding. They were first mentioned in John Constable's "Letter to the Editor of the Spirit of the Times," which describes a trip guided by Higby in 1843. Constable noted that Higby's boat weighed about ninety pounds, was made of cedar, and could be carried by one man yet was capable of holding three people and all their supplies. In all likelihood, Higby's boats were small rowboats sometimes called "carry boats." Such

1. For more information on Higby, see Pilcher, *The Constables*, 49–51.

homemade carry boats were a precursor of the iconic Adirondack guideboat.[2]

McEntee describes Higby in detail in his journal. Interestingly, he chose not to describe any of the four men Higby was guiding. He does note that the last names of two of the sportsmen were "Doig" and "Murray." He recorded nothing at all about the other two. The two parties camped together for a week. During that time, McEntee must have learned their full names, their professions, and something of their families, but he apparently felt these details did not merit mention in the journal. This tendency continues throughout the rest of the journal. McEntee rarely recorded conversations and provided full names for and extended descriptions of only a few of the other people he met.

Even when camped in close quarters with others at Smith's Lake, Raquette Lake, and Blue Mountain Lake, McEntee and Tubby appear not to have spent much time socializing with the other travelers they met. The only time any of these other campers joined their party for a joint adventure was for the climb up Blue Mountain, described in letter 20. McEntee obviously did not embark on the trip to make new friends. His focus always remained fixed on making sketches of unique, interesting landscapes that he could later use as the basis for paintings.

2. Stephen B. Sulavik, *The Adirondack Guideboat: Its Origins, Its Builders, and Their Boats*, with revisions and additions by Edward Comstock Jr. and Christopher H. Woodward (Peterborough, NH: Bauhan, 2018), 44–45.

Impressions of Smith's Lake

To Mr. & Mrs. James S. McEntee, Clovertop, Rondout, New York
Sunday, June 22, 1851

Dear Mother, dear Father,

After we left O'Kane's, we paddled upstream on the winding Beaver for two blissful warm, clear days until we came to a set of shallow rapids. We camped there for the night, but the punkies and mosquitos were so thick we moved to a better camp at a lake a few miles further upstream.

I am sending a separate letter to Gussie about that camp and about meeting a party of four at Albany Lake guided by Higbie. This past Wednesday all of us continued upstream, through another rapid to beautiful Smith's Lake. While Joe and I went for a swim, Joe's dog ran off but returned on his own after we fruitlessly stumbled through the bushes for half an hour looking for him. He is a good companion, but he is more trouble than Joe anticipated. Puffer has agreed to take him back to his farm and keep him there until I can fetch him after the trip.

We are now staying in a fine camp built this past spring by Higbie. It is well situated, has good water and even a covered outdoor table with split-log benches where we take our meals. Our plan is to remain here for about two weeks. In a few days Puffer will return to town with the Higbie party then return to us with fresh supplies. I am sending a pack of letters with him and have given him strict orders to bring in our letters and some newspapers.

I had heard much about the sublime beauty of this place from Sylvester. I thought he must be exaggerating, but as we paddled up the lake on the day we arrived, we all agreed it was one of the fairest scenes we had ever laid eyes upon. Even stolid Puffer was moved

THE DEER BY THE BRINK.

1.5. Jervis McEntee, *Deer by the Brink*, wood engraving by Loomis-Annin from sketch by Jervis McEntee. In McEntee, "The Lakes of the Wilderness," 338. Courtesy of the American Antiquarian Society, Worcester, MA.

to remark he wished he was an artist so he could try to capture the beauty of the place.

We began sketching the next morning from a point near camp. Hoping to get a better view we paddled out into the lake a little way. Suddenly the wind came up and lashed the previously calm waters into crashing waves. We were at their mercy as we had only one paddle. I found a loose board in the bottom of the boat but it proved of little help. Higbie spied our trouble and hurried to our aid with a proper paddle and we made our way safely back to shore.

That evening the persistent wind finally stopped. "The hills on the opposite shore appeared clothed in a thin blue haze, softened by the afternoon shadows emitting from the lake. The forest stretched away into the distance, almost blending with the faint misty peaks of the Adirondacks that appear over the tops of the trees on the pine island. Finally, before us the lake was still, and their summits were reflected in it, forming a picture of surpassing beauty. We felt too much elated by the sight, and taking the boat, we rowed down the lake in search of points to take sketches."

We have spent most of every day since hard at the artist's favored work. We found an excellent vantage point on a small island. I have completed several good sketches, including a fine one in color of a salmon trout caught by Puffer. I have commenced a large sketch of the forest by the outlet that I plan to finish in the next few days.

It is difficult to capture the scene here in words. "The sunsets are unlike any we might see at home. Last evening was cloudy with rain but on Friday the sun set clear, throwing his soft golden light over the fringed hilltops, making deeper the shadows that hung round their sides. Delicate violet clouds floated in the golden air, and their fair forms were imaged back from the quiet waters." I hope this pencil sketch may convey some of the beauty of this place to you.

Your grateful son,
Jervis

Notes for Letter 9

In the years between 1845 and 1890, a steady flow of sportsmen had Smith's Lake as their destination. Their guides built semipermanent camps at several locations around the lake to shelter the groups they expected in any given season. These camps typically consisted of lean-tos or even enclosed cabins as well as camp furniture such as tables, benches, and dining shelters—all constructed of logs, bark, and branches. Typically, guides' camps would overlook the lake near springs of freshwater.[1] McEntee's journal provides scant description of the Higby camp where they stayed, save for the fact that it had a sand beach and a good spring with a spout for filling containers. Based on hints from various journal entries, it can be surmised that the camp was probably located on the west shore not too far from the outlet.

Smith's Lake and the small streams that flow into it form the headwaters of the Beaver River. McEntee's description of its sublime beauty has been echoed by every visitor since he was there. One of its main attractions for fishermen was the fact that it was deep and cold enough to support a sizable population of lake trout. These fish, called "salmon trout" back in those days, could reach lengths of twenty inches or more and were extremely tasty. To catch these deepwater fish, guides would anchor floats in locations where they were known to gather. Weighted fishing lines dropped at these marked spots usually resulted in a catch. McEntee praised the beauty of these fish and carefully made a color sketch of one. That sketch, like most of the rest of the sketches he made on the trip, has not been located or has not survived.

1. Smith's Lake was consistently mentioned as a preferred Adirondack destination in numerous articles that appeared in the national sporting magazine *Forest and Stream* and was a recommended destination in successive editions of Edwin Wallace's *Descriptive Guide to the Adirondacks: And Handbook of Travel to Saratoga Springs, Schroon Lake, Lakes Luzerne, George, and Champlain, the Ausable Chasm, the Thousand Islands, Massena Springs and Trenton Falls*, published from 1872 to 1897, first by Columbian Book in Hartford, Connecticut, and thereafter by W. Gill in Syracuse, New York.

Smith's Lake continued to attract considerable numbers of sportsmen until 1891. By that time, there were several established guides' camps along its shores as well as a rustic hotel on the west side, possibly near the site where the old Higby camp once stood. Then in 1891 Dr. William Seward Webb acquired the land surrounding Smith's Lake. Webb was well aware of the lake's reputation as a famous destination of old-time sportsmen. He set aside forty thousand acres surrounding Smith's Lake from his other lands, closed that area off to the public, and created his own private wilderness park where he could entertain his wealthy friends.

Webb named his private preserve "Nehasane Park" after the original Mohawk name for the Beaver River. As a tribute to his wife, Elisa "Lila" Vanderbilt, he renamed Smith's Lake "Lake Lila."[2] Webb is perhaps best remembered in Adirondack history as the person who financed and supervised the building of a railroad that connected the Mohawk Valley with Montreal.[3]

2. For details about Webb's Nehasane Park, see Harvey H. Kaiser, *Great Camps of the Adirondacks*, rev. ed. (Jaffrey, NH: David R. Godine, 2020), 183–87, and Gladys Montgomery, *An Elegant Wilderness: Great Camps and Grand Lodges of the Adirondacks, 1855–1935* (New York: Acanthus Press, 2011), 110–21.

3. The impact of that railroad on the upper Beaver River area is discussed in my book *Beaver River Country*, 98–104.

The Hermit David Smith's Cabin

To Mr. Frederic E. Church, the American
Art-Union Bldg., New York, New York
Sunday, June 22, 1851

Dear Mr. Church,

Joseph Tubby and I arrived here at beautiful Smith's Lake on
Wednesday the 18th. We are encamped in a snug shanty with a lean-
to roof in a fine camp constructed just this year by a famous woods
guide named Higbie. The camp has a clear spring and a sand beach.
From a little point nearby, we have fine views of the lake, forest and
surrounding low mountains.

Our first two days here were spent exploring about the lake looking for the best views to sketch. Although it is often windy, the days
have been mostly dry, with thunderstorms restricted to the nights
and evenings. We caught several very large salmon trout using a
method taught us by our guide. When we next meet, I shall show
you the color sketch I made of the largest of these fish, fully twenty
inches long, caught by Puffer.

On Friday, Joe and I set up our outdoor studio on a small island
near the outlet of the lake. I commenced a picture that features a
view of the dense, dark woods set in contrast to the bright water and
an open marsh with a few wildflowers. We returned to the island yesterday. I am pleased with how my sketch is developing and can easily
envision it in oils. I believe I am beginning to truly appreciate your
suggestion of traveling the wilderness for artistic inspiration.

We spent the morning today rowing a short way up the lake in
order to climb a small mountain with the hope of getting a view
over the whole area. We landed in a sheltered spot at the base of the

mountain where there is a clearing of a few acres. This clearing was made twenty years ago by a man of the name of Smith for whom the lake was named and who lived here fifteen years entirely alone. We came upon the ruins of his cabin, built with logs and covered with long split shingles, and "as I looked upon his deserted hearthstone where he sat and mused alone, I regretted that the poor old man was compelled to leave. He went away almost five years ago to seek a home in the far west. About that time fishing parties began to visit the lake quite frequently, which I suppose was an annoyance to him who had come so far in the forest and borne away so many discomforts for the sake of being alone."

"The spot which he cleared had grown up with a thrifty growth of wild cherry trees from ten to twenty feet in height, among which we found one solitary apple tree, a fitting type among this dissolution of him who planted it there. The trailing vine matted in wild luxuriance overran his fields and trees were growing where his spade had turned up the dark, rich mold."

We explored his ruined cabin, then followed the trail to the hilltop beaten down by the boots of frequent visitors. The hill is five hundred to six hundred feet high with good views. Joe and I hope to return with our sketching boxes sometime this coming week.

I do hope you will permit me to visit you with my box of sketches when I next return to New York City. Your advice and encouragement have powered my belief that I am on the proper course to becoming an artist. It is my fondest wish that we can continue our artistic association in the future.

Sincerely, your friend,

Jervis McEntee

Notes for Letter 10

The journal describes how McEntee and Tubby rowed around Smith's Lake seeking the best scenes to sketch. They spent several days sketching from an island near the outlet. *The National Academy of Design, Exhibition Record, 1826–1860*, volume 2, reveals that in 1852 McEntee exhibited a painting of the northern forest near the outlet of Smith's Lake.[1] Since this painting is not known to exist still, in this letter the brief description of what it might have shown is an invention based on my own visit to the same location.

McEntee's journal records that he and Tubby visited David Smith's abandoned cabin on June 22. They climbed Smith's Mountain, now named Mount Frederica, the same day. Although McEntee remarked on the fine view, there is no record that either he or Tubby ever made sketches from the summit. McEntee likely gathered his information about Smith from Asa Puffer, who would have briefly met Smith in 1841 during Nelson Beach's survey for the Carthage–to–Lake Champlain Road. Beach hired Smith to help find a route for the road around the Stillwater section of the Beaver River. According to Beach's journal, Smith left the surveying team after only three days.[2] Smith was tasked with delivering a load of supplies to the survey team at Long Lake, but he and the supplies never arrived. By 1845, Smith had abandoned his homestead on the beautiful lake named for him.

There are no existing first-person accounts of David Smith. The most reliable published account is by Nathaniel Bartlett Sylvester in *Historical Sketches of Northern New York and the Adirondack Wilderness* (1877).[3] According to Sylvester, David Smith is presumed to have arrived along the upper Beaver River sometime in the late 1820s. At first, he built a shanty at Stillwater near where O'Kane later settled.

1. Jervis McEntee, *A View in the Forest of Northern New York—Outlet of Smith's Lake* (1852), listed in *National Academy of Design Exhibition Record, 1826–1860*, 2 vols., comp. Mary Bartlett Cowdrey (New York: New-York Historical Society, 1943), 2:15.

2. Beach, "Journal of Proceedings Relative to the Carthage and Lake Champlain Road," entries for June 4 and 10, 1841.

3. Sylvester, *Historical Sketches of Northern New York*, 129–31.

To avoid having his solitude interrupted by the infrequent hunter or trapper, Smith moved farther upstream around 1830, where he cleared a few acres and built a cabin on the bank of the secluded lake at the headwaters of the Beaver River. Local hunters and fisherman came to call that lake "Smith's Lake," and the name stuck.

This letter describing the sketches McEntee was making at Smith's Lake includes the suggestion that Church might meet him after the trip. In fact, McEntee and Church occasionally socialized after the trip and eventually became lifelong friends. In later years, they went on sketching trips together, and on one occasion Church paid McEntee's expenses to join him on a sketching trip to Mexico. After McEntee's death in January 1891, Church wrote a condolence letter to the McEntee family in which he described McEntee as "a man pure, upright, and as modest as he was gifted."[4]

4. Frederic E. Church to "Miss McEntee," Jan. 30, 1891, in Lee E. Vedder, curator, *Jervis McEntee: Painter-Poet of the Hudson River School*, catalog, exhibition Aug. 25–Dec. 13, 2015 (New Paltz, NY: Samuel Dorsky Museum of Art, State Univ. of New York, 2015), 113.

Conflicted Feelings about Hunting

To Miss Julia McEntee, c/o Mr. Charles McEntee,
Rondout, New York
Monday, June 23, 1851

Dear Cousin Julia,

You asked before I left on this trip why I worried so much about the type of gun I planned to bring along. I answered hastily that I expected to need a proper weapon because I would be hunting wild game for our dinner. Now that I have gained some little experience with the reality of carrying a firearm into the wilderness, I am prepared to give you a more thoughtful answer.

Before the trip I obtained a fine double-barrel shotgun from a Rondout gunsmith recommended by my father. He assured me of its effectiveness at short range against all manner of game, especially birds. The gun is furnished with a rugged cover intended to protect it from the worst weather. When Joe heard what I had bought, he promptly borrowed a similar gun from a friend, although devoid of a cover.

As I had very little prior experience with hunting, I was unsure of how I would feel about killing animals and birds for our dinners. Of course, there is a sort of excitement that naturally arises from encountering a wild creature that might serve as a later meal. On our first day out of Lowville Joe and I each tried our luck at shooting, and after many a missed mark we managed together to kill a half-dozen pigeons. I felt a sense of real pride when I made a present of them to Mrs. Fenton.

Later that day while we rested our weary legs, Puffer went a short distance into the forest in search of a deer for our supper. We presently heard his rifle crack. He reappeared carrying a sleek young deer that he threw in the wagon with our baggage. I could not help but feel a strong pang of regret at the necessity of killing such a beautiful creature for meat.

Since the first day I have repeatedly felt the pull of these contrary emotions—the excitement of the hunt and the regret at the consequence. Joe seems not to feel as I do and daily asks Puffer to show him better means to shoot a deer, a feat he has not yet accomplished. I killed a single deer on a night hunt with Puffer, or at least I think I did. Puffer fired at the same animal at the same time but assured me it was my shot that sealed its fate.

Initially I did not feel conflicted about shooting birds. When we first arrived at Albany Lake, I shot at two black ducks but missed. As I tried to quickly reload, I dropped my ramrod overboard. Fortunately, the water was shallow and we soon recovered it. As it was Sunday, I wondered afterward if this was a message from Providence about my thoughtlessly trying to destroy a creature that I had no intention of eating.

An event last evening conclusively settled the matter for me. "While sitting by the fire at dusk some owls flew into the trees that stood near, and I, seizing my gun, shot one. I afterwards regretted doing so as the rest of the owls hovered near and expressed their sorrow for their lost companion by a low and melancholy whistling. I repent that I had destroyed the life even of an owl so wantonly and promised myself that in the future I would be more considerate. I am inclined to think that animals feel as keenly as we do the loss of a companion." Henceforth my gun will be silent except in case of true need for sustenance. I find that no such moral wrestling is required for fishing, so I shall bend my diet in the piscatory direction.

Puffer may well leave camp tomorrow to secure needed supplies from town. I amused myself this afternoon by decorating and converting an empty shot bag into a fancy mail bag so Puffer can carry all of my letters and those Joe has written safely together to the post office. Please send me your thoughts as Puffer will be picking up my mail in Lowville again later in July.

Fondly, your cousin,
Jervis

Notes for Letter 11

This letter reflecting McEntee's feelings about killing an owl and his ambivalence about hunting in general is based on his journal entry of June 24, not June 23. Because Puffer left for town before noon on June 24, for this event to appear in a letter that Puffer took with him, it was necessary to rearrange the dates slightly.

That McEntee expressed any doubts about hunting is remarkable. From the first day of the trip, although he mentioned sadness that it was necessary to kill so beautiful an animal as a deer for food, this feeling didn't keep him from firing on a fair number of birds until the owl incident. In contrast, most sportsmen during the rest of the nineteenth century and well into the twentieth century traveled to the Adirondacks with the explicit purpose of hunting white-tailed deer. Their impact on wildlife was limited in the years before the Civil War, however, because of the guns they used.

The guns produced in those early days were not made in factories but by gunsmiths. They were muzzle-loading flintlocks that included smooth-barreled muskets, shotguns, and the more accurate grooved-barrel rifles. Shotguns designed primary for shooting birds on the wing were called "fowling pieces." They were single-shot weapons that took significant time to reload because they required a ramrod to push the gunpowder and shot down the barrel. If McEntee had not retrieved the ramrod he dropped overboard, his gun would have been useless.

These shotguns had a somewhat restricted range and were inaccurate in the hands of a novice. A good rifle in the hands of an experienced hunter was much more effective. It is significant that both McEntee and Tubby used shotguns and appear to have killed only one deer apiece during two months in the wilderness. Puffer used a rifle. McEntee recorded Puffer killed at least fifteen deer during the trip. It was not unusual for an Adirondack guide to fire at a deer simultaneously with the sportsman, then disingenuously claim the sportsman had made the kill.

The journal does not record that either McEntee or Tubby ever killed another animal after leaving Smith's Lake, although they occasionally accompanied Puffer while he hunted. For the remainder of the trip, all the venison they ate was supplied by Puffer's rifle. As noted in the letter, both McEntee and Tubby fished nearly every day. Neither ever expressed any qualms about eating fish. Eight years after the trip, when retelling the story in "The Lakes of the Wilderness" in 1859, McEntee claimed that they did not bring guns along so much for hunting or to "shoot at every creature that happened to cross our path" but to avoid feeling "spooney [sic]"—that is, foolish.[1]

Hunting for sport increased significantly after the Civil War. Many veterans returned home with guns they acquired in the army. The mass production of firearms in factories also made guns more generally available. Flintlocks were displaced by rifles with cartridges, which made firing more reliable and reloading quicker. The introduction of the Spencer repeating carbine in 1860 and the Winchester rifle in 1873 made hunting more feasible for amateur sportsmen.[2] Although the number of hunters increased, the Adirondack deer population did not suffer because logging and forest fires had opened up the forest canopy and promoted growth of the browse deer favored.[3]

1. McEntee, "Lakes of the Wilderness," 336.

2. Philip Schreier, "History of the Hunting Rifle in America," *American Hunter* (NRA), May 16, 2015, https://www.americanhunter.org/content/history-of-the -hunting-rifle-in-america/.

3. See Philip G. Terrie, *Wildlife and Wilderness: A History of Adirondack Mammals* (Bovina Center, NY: Purple Mountain Press, 1993), 87.

Excerpts from McEntee's Journal, "Sick, Tired and Hungry"

June 24–July 2, 1851

The ten days between the afternoon of June 24 and the morning of July 2 proved to be a low point in the trip. McEntee's journal does not record any letters being written about events during this interval. To fill in the story, here's a summary of those days accompanied by verbatim extracts from McEntee's journal.

On June 24, the four Lowville men guided by Higby decided to return to town because the fishing was not going well. Puffer left with them. He needed to get fresh provisions for the next part of the trip. To leave a boat for McEntee and Tubby, Puffer traveled with the Higby party, which had two boats, each of which could carry three men. Puffer agreed to take Tubby's dog along to his farm and keep it until after the trip.

"We regretted parting with them, for by camping together we had become quite intimately acquainted, and with as such company it did not seem as though we were so far back in the forest."

This departure left McEntee and Tubby alone at Higby's camp at Smith's Lake. McEntee was initially optimistic about him and Joe spending time by themselves.

"Thus, were we left alone in the forest and as far from feeling lonely, we enjoyed ourselves in a more quiet manner and realized that satisfaction of being alone and afar from the hurried tumult of the world of trade and business that we had come so far to find."

His optimism was short-lived. Their stock of food was limited, so they needed to catch fish to supplement their remaining supply of flour, rice, and beans. On June 25, they fished all day but caught nothing. McEntee took on the task of making something for dinner.

"I officiated as cook and together we got up some strange dishes by exercising and carrying into effect the suggestions of our combined imagination. For supper we boiled some rice and made some rice cakes which we baked in the frying pan. I had to mix some flour with them in order to make them hang together."

Both agreed they tasted good but would have been better if they had butter. McEntee imagined that his friends would be amused to see him trying to cook over an open fire. The next day, June 26, they went fishing again, but, again, did not catch any fish.

"We got lots of bites from punkies but not one from trout, and disheartened and discouraged we started for camp. Just before we got to Smith's clearing a dark cloud which came over the hill began to rain down upon our devoted heads. We paddled with all our might and hauling our boat on shore at the clearing scrambled up through the brush and wet bushes to Smith's old log house. Here we had tolerable shelter but the omnipresent punkies forced us to set up a 'smudge' and filling the crazy old cabin with dense smoke we compelled them to evacuate. We stayed here perhaps a half hour when the rain ceased and we went on our way to our camp. While we were here, we both of us remarked a dull feeling in our head."

They ate some leftover rice cakes, then spent the rest of the afternoon lying in the shanty. McEntee's headache got worse. By nightfall he was in so much pain that he had trouble sleeping. Both were still sick the morning of June 27.

"I awoke again on the morrow weak and unfit for any duty. Joe was in the same state, and together we are where [sic] a sorry couple to be alone in the woods fifty miles from any civilization."

Around noon a party of six local sportsmen led by Squire Snell (his first name was Squire), a surveyor who knew Puffer, stopped at their camp and conversed with the artists for half an hour before moving on. McEntee and Tubby tried to sketch later that afternoon, but they still lacked the necessary concentration. During the evening, they talked about how much they wished Puffer would return and rescue them from their predicament. Their spirits were low, and both were "fighting against melancholy." They again slept poorly.

"In the afternoon we took our sketching boxes and went over to work on our view of the outlet. We were so weak and felt so stupid that we could not do much and we stayed only until about 4 o'clock. We whiled away the remaining hours of the day [with] pleasant conversation concerning Puffer's return. How glad we would be to see him, how we would feast upon the good things which he was to bring with him, and how our hearts were to be [illegible] by the good long letters from home of which he was to be the bearer."

On Saturday, June 28, after a warm breakfast, probably oatmeal, they began to feel better. They were able to work on the sketches they had started two days earlier, although not without mishap.

"Getting into our boat we paddled down to the outlet and fixing places for seats upon a large pine tree that had fallen into the stream we commenced a sketch. The punkies began to annoy us so that we had to build a smudge in a log, which set it on fire, placing us in imminent danger of being precipitated, with our boxes, into the stream."

They returned to camp and rested. That evening they felt better and sang some old songs around the campfire. McEntee, ever the optimist, noted, "We were getting stronger and began to feel in better spirits, although we had not suffered ourselves to get the blues but rather joked and made sport about our misfortune."

McEntee cooked the usual shortcake for breakfast on Sunday, June 29, "made thin and baked hard." Their need for fresh food was great, so they went fishing, this time with a little better luck.

"It was the Sabbath but we thought it was no sin to go fishing since we had nothing in the meat line for our dinner and our improving appetites craved more substantial stuff than we possessed in camp. . . . I caught two good sized speckled trout, enough for our dinner, and the fish being decidedly dull about biting we started for home after fishing in three or four different places."

In the afternoon, Tubby broke the handle of the hatchet getting firewood but was able to fashion a new one from a branch. They again discussed how much they looked forward to Puffer's return.

"We read a little and passed the remainder of the afternoon until suppertime in cheerful talk, mostly relating to Puffer's arrival, to which we were anxiously looking forward."

On June 30, their headaches returned, so they stayed in camp all day.

"We had frequent showers during the day so that we were unable to work on our sketches from the outlet."

On Tuesday, July 1, they finally felt a bit better. They rowed around the lake for a while, looking for new views to sketch. McEntee admitted he did not feel very strong, having not eaten much lately. Suddenly a strong storm caught them out in the middle of the lake.

"We headed our boat for a bare rock in the lake and paddled with all our might; for down came the rain enveloping the land in a misty shroud and its feet pattered upon the waves which the wind accompanying it was rolling up furiously. We reach[ed] the rock before the heaviest of the storm reached us and hauling our boat hastily up . . . we sat down on some loose stones placing ourselves in the smallest possible compass and covering over us our umbrellas which fortunately we had brought with us."

"We were pretty tired when we arrived at the camp as well as hungry[;] in placing some beans over the fire to boil we threw ourselves down in the cabin and waited anxiously for them to cook."

They had heard a rifle shot that morning. McEntee surmised that it was Puffer signaling that he was nearby and would be back in camp the next day.

"In the evening we sat before the fire on our camp stools and talked upon the pleasing subject of Puffer's return. We had heard in the morning what we took to be a rifle shot and had been watching the outlet all day until now it had grown dark and he had not come we contented ourselves with talking about him."

The prospect of Puffer's return cheered them but also made them homesick. They talked about the letters from home they hoped to get. Of course, they thought of all their favorite foods. One of their chief regrets was that by taking the trip they had deprived themselves of the fruit puddings and pies they would have been eating at home. Then they choked down leftover beans for supper. To cap off an already hard day, they ran out of wood during a cold night.

On Wednesday morning, July 2, after another pancake breakfast, Tubby went out to sketch, while McEntee stayed in camp trying to repair his boots with some small nails he found.

"I stayed in camp to 'heal' my boots which were of late become very upside down, the heels having so far forgotten their avocation as to begin to sneak from duty by turning up."

It wasn't long before they heard Puffer's gun sounding from the beach. They hurried to help him carry up the new supplies. Puffer also had a stack of letters, including a long one from McEntee's sister Gussie, and some newspapers.

"[We] commended Puffer over and over again for bringing each article which we had forgotten to send for and in short we were so perfectly elated that he had got back with us again that we were unable to find the words to express our happiness."

Puffer cooked them the first proper dinner they had had in ten days. After dinner, they joked about the fact that many people in Lowville did not think they would survive very long in the woods. They were in such high spirits that McEntee got out his flask, and they had a drink. McEntee noted that he felt like dancing about the camp, but he restrained himself. During the remainder of the trip, they never doubted how essential Puffer was to their happiness.

Notes for the Journal Excerpts

Inspired by Joel Headley's glowing account of his trips in *The Adirondack; Or, Life in the Woods* (1849), McEntee and Tubby had romantic expectations of how well they would fare in the wilderness. During the first twelve days of the trip, their experience generally lived up to their expectations, thanks largely to the efforts of their guide, Asa Puffer. When Puffer left camp on June 24 to fetch additional supplies, however, the reality of being on their own miles from town finally set in. Over the next ten days, they had to deal with illness, little food, poor luck in fishing, bad weather, clouds of insects, and a few mishaps that fortunately did them no serious injury.

McEntee described the illness they suffered at Smith's Lake as consisting of severe headaches and fatigue. These symptoms could have been caused by their poor diet, contaminated drinking water, or the inhalation of the smoke they frequently sat in to drive off insects.

The group of six local men from Martinsburg who stopped briefly to converse with the artists on June 27 included Squire H. Snell. A surveyor by trade, Snell was quite familiar with the upper Beaver River. He would also have known Puffer since they had worked together with Nelson Beach in laying out the Carthage–to–Lake Champlain Road in 1841. He later worked for Verplanck Colvin as head of the northwest division of the Adirondack Survey.

In the notes to letter 5, I remarked that the condition of McEntee's boots would be a reoccurring theme. The boots McEntee chose to wear are emblematic of his lack of experience in outdoor life. They may have been stylish, but by this point in the trip they not only hurt his feet but also started to fall apart. His repairs would not last long.

The Forgotten Bag and the Constable Camp on Raquette Lake

To Mr. Jervis McEntee and Mr. Joseph Tubby,
Higby Camp, Smith's Lake
Saturday, June 28, 1851

Dear Jervis and Joe,

I am writing this letter in haste while Asa Puffer waits to carry it to you. Puffer came to my rooms today. I was expecting him as he left word for me at my office yesterday informing me that he had returned to town to secure supplies and retrieve your mail. I gave him your forgotten carpetbag.

I was not much surprised by your letter of June 12 from Fenton's. I well remember how anxious you were to be on your way after so many days of idleness. The same day I received your letter, I made haste to your inn as I wanted to take possession of your bag before it was misplaced by the landlord. The landlord had not yet discovered the bag, so we searched your room together and found it on a shelf in the back of the wardrobe.

Your bag has since occupied a place of honor behind the door of my rooms. I am glad to be able to send it on its way at last. At your request, I fully intended to send it to you earlier with Higby's party. I wrote to both Higby and Doig asking them to fetch the bag, but neither ever appeared.

You will also be glad to know that about a week after you departed for Smith's Lake, I received a kind letter from Mr. John Constable of Constable Hall. He was replying to my letter on your behalf requesting permission for you to camp for two weeks this coming month at his open camp on Raquette Lake. He is glad to have you there but asks that you vacate no later than July 25, when he expects to arrive with his family and remain for the month of August. As a courtesy, I suggest you have Puffer replenish the firewood supply on your departure.

I have not visited the Constable camp myself but know that Higby built it with great care only last year. He tells me it is located on a point at the prettiest spot on the lake. It has the advantage of a good spring of excellent water. I'm sure it will meet your artistic needs. Higby was with the Constable women last summer when they climbed Blue Mountain and carved their initials on a blasted tree near the top. Perhaps he already told you of this adventure. I understand Higby will be guiding for the Constables again this summer.

I have had no reply from William Wood to my letter sent now two months ago. This need not trouble you as Wood always stands prepared to assist every party that arrives at the Raquette. I feel certain he will have a boat you can borrow. Wood knows about when to expect your arrival, and Puffer knows how to summon Wood to your aid. You will find Wood will be helpful to you in many small ways.

Thank you for your invitation to join you for a few days, but the press of business prevents me leaving for the woods at any time this season. If I can be of any further service, please write.

Your friend,

Nathaniel B. Sylvester

Notes for Letter 12

This letter is intended to explain a few items not explicitly addressed in McEntee's journal but necessary for understanding future events. It begins with my fanciful explanation of the fate of McEntee's forgotten bag.[1] Although McEntee's journal records his disappointment that the Higby party did not bring the bag, it does not explicitly mention that Puffer returned to Smith's Lake with the forgotten bag. Yet his general excitement about all the things Puffer did bring suggests the previously forgotten bag was among them.

It was established earlier that Nathaniel Sylvester assisted in the planning of the sketching trip. Part of that plan would likely have been to alert John Constable of McEntee's desire to use the Constable open camp at Raquette Lake for two weeks during July. Strictly speaking, permission would not have been required, but as the Constable family was quite prominent and possibly Sylvester's client, such a request would have been wise. As noted in this letter, the Constable family did vacation at Constable Point later in July 1851, guided by Higby.

The Constable family was one of the wealthiest in the north country. William Constable Sr. had acquired title to nearly all the northern Adirondacks in 1792 as a partner in the Macomb Purchase. His son, William Constable Jr., inherited about ten townships of the Macomb Purchase that had not yet been sold by 1807. William Jr. married Mary Eliza McVicker in 1810, and the couple decided to build a home in the north country to better oversee land sales. William Jr. was badly injured while supervising construction of Constable Hall in 1819. He never fully recovered from this injury and died in 1821. At age thirty-two, Mary Eliza McVicker was left to raise their five children on her own.

In the summer of 1850, the five Constable siblings and some close friends took a month-long camping trip to Raquette Lake. There were thirteen in the party, seven women and six men. William Higby was

1. See letter 4 of June 12 to Nathaniel Sylvester.

their guide. He constructed two open lean-tos on a point reaching out from the south shore, one for the men and one for the women, separated by a decent distance for privacy. Stout boards were ordered to be delivered from Long Lake to construct tables and seats.[2]

2. More details on the Constable family camping trips are provided in part two, and even more detail can be found in Pilcher, *The Constables*.

Part Two | Raquette Lake

**Smith's Lake to Brandreth Lake to Raquette Lake
to Blue Mountain Lake to Long Lake**

July 3:   By boat on Shingle Shanty Brook, then by foot and carrying/
             bushwhacking to the Shingle Shanty along the Carthage-to–
             Lake Champlain Road—about 10 miles total

July 5:   On foot on road from the Shingle Shanty to Brandreth Lake—
             2.5 miles

July 6:   By wagon and on foot from Brandreth Lake to Raquette Lake,
             then by boat to Wood's cabin—10 miles, including 3.5 miles
             by boat

July 7:   By boat across the lake to the Constable family open camp

July 21–22: On foot by road to Austin's farm on Long Lake and return—
             32 miles round trip

July 23:   By boat on Marion River from Raquette Lake to Blue
             Mountain Lake—14 miles, with short carries

July 26:   Hike and carry on a hunter's trail from Blue Mountain Lake to
             Austin's farm on Long Lake—6 miles

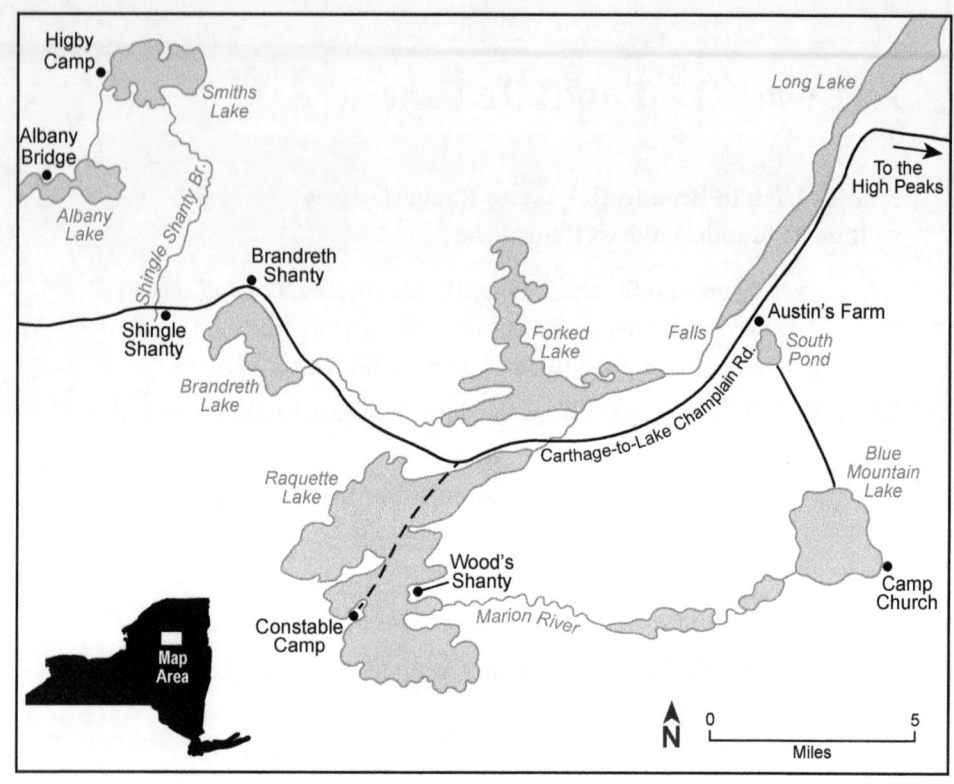

M.2. Map for part two. Joseph W. Stoll, Syracuse University Cartographic Laboratory.

Difficult Journey to the Shingle Shanty

To Mr. and Mrs. John Tubby, Rondout, Ulster County, New York
Rackett Lake, July 10, [1851]

Dear Friends,

The last letter I wrote to you was from Smith's Lake, which place we left a week ago today for Beach's Lake, where we arrived last Saturday.

We had a great time getting up the Beaver River. We left in two boats: Puffer in one with provisions and Jerv and I in another with our knapsacks and sketching boxes. While crossing Smith's Lake we saw a deer on the shore which Puffer started for, but the gentleman left on suspicion. The Beaver River up here is but a small stream hardly large enough to go up with a boat and as crooked as a drunken man's track. We saw a fish hawk's nest on a large pine and kept in sight of that for a long time. Sometimes we passed it and then the stream took a turn back (as Dodge used to say to Mr. Fisher) 'til we were very near the same place again.

After we had got a short distance up, we heard a great noise in the alders which Puffer who was ahead of us said was a moose. He saw his horns above the tops of the alders but was not near enough to fire. Puffer kept ahead of us to shoot the deer as he could paddle upstream without making any noise, and they are so very watchful that the slightest noise alarms them. He shot two very fine ones on his way up which Jerv and I are going to have dressed for rugs to put in our rooms.

It was very tiresome paddling in so narrow and winding stream and in some places we had to get out and haul the boat by hand. We went 'til we came to the south branch and took that as we had been told it would take us within ½ mile of the place we wanted to get to that night. It was a mere ditch at the mouth. The alders grew so that in some places they met across the stream and we had to pull through them instead of paddling, but after a while we came to a place where it was wider and deeper so we made better headway. After some hours paddling, we came again to shoal water and had to wade and draw the boat, and to add to our pleasure the rain came down in good earnest and soaked us through.

We now got to a place where the stream again divided and did not know which one to take as Puffer had never been up this branch, but we took the one to the right and such an abominable place cannot be found in the world as this was. The punkies were thicker there, but there is no use trying to think of anything to compare to them. To give them their due, they filled our eyes and covered our faces and hands. It was raining also quite hard and our boat was in a fix. She had got on a log and I jumped out into what I supposed to be 6 to 8 inches of water, and so it was but there was about 3 feet of mud with it of the softest kind. Jerv sat in the stern of the boat laughing to split at my disappearing so suddenly, in which I had to join, but I could not get the boat off alone, so he had to get out with me and suffer in the same righteous cause.

We got her out of this strait but only to get into another for there was more logs across the stream, so we got out on the bank and joined Puffer who was a few rods further up, where we packed our things and covered them over with our tent to keep the rain off and made up a good fire and dried ourselves. The fire also drives the punkies away, so that we felt quite comfortable.

About 6 o'clock we left for the road through the woods steering south. We had got completely turned around since morning, that is Jerv and myself. We thought south was north and imagined our guide was wrong, but when the compass told us we found it was just as he said. About an hour and a half walk over swamp and hill and fallen logs took us to the road about a mile from what is called the Shingle Shanty, but when we got there, we found there was not much of a shanty left, but there was enough to keep us dry, and after making a hardy supper and putting on other clothes we went to sleep.

LEAVING THE BOATS.

2.1. Jervis McEntee, *Leaving the Boats*, wood engraving by Loomis-Annin from sketch by Jervis McEntee. In Jervis McEntee, "The Lakes of the Wilderness," *Great Republic Monthly*, Apr. 1, 1859, 342. Courtesy of the American Antiquarian Society, Worcester, MA.

Next morning, which was the glorious fourth, we went down to our boats for the remainder of our things. We followed the Beaver River to see if we could get up with our traps in the boat any nearer to where we were, but it was so crooked and shallow that it took us over three hours to get to the place we walked from the night before in half that time.

We packed our things and got ready to start. I had a butter tub or firkin filled with groceries and weighing I suppose at starting about 50 pounds. Jerv had our sketching boxes, umbrellas, camp stools and guns. Puffer made a pack of the tent, filling it with everything we wanted to take and such a load he had it was almost as much as I

THE SHINGLE SHANTY.

2.2. Jervis McEntee, *The Shingle Shanty*, wood engraving by Loomis-Annin from sketch by Jervis McEntee. In McEntee, "The Lakes of the Wilderness," 343. Courtesy of the American Antiquarian Society, Worcester, MA.

could get from the ground. It was raining and the bushes were wet. Our loads were heavy, and it took us about two hours and a half to get back. But after all it was rather a pleasant fourth. It would have been a great deal more so if the weather had been fine, which I hope it was with you.

After we got back to the shanty, we cooked our dinner and got talking about home and wondering what you had for dinner. I thought it was likely a current pudding and I wish I had about half a one such as we used to have out there as I think I could stow that much away quite easy. I am going to try my hand at making one very soon. The currents here are hardly ripe enough. The raspberries are in blossom yet and we have not had a night yet that we could not sleep with our blankets wrapped around us and a good fire in front.

I received a letter from James without any news of any account with the exception of the Elmendorfs having bought my picture, which was first rate news. When he writes again, let him fill it up with anything, as any kind of news is new out here. How comes in the berries? How many have you sold? Tell mother she must hold herself in readiness to make a good damson pudding as good as one as she can make as I have been bragging to Jerv about it and he is coming to try one as soon as they are fit. We intend to go through to Lake George and come home by way of Albany, but I cannot tell the time exactly. When you write again direct it to Joseph Tubby artist, Adirondack, New York. Puffer goes in tomorrow to Lowville for Josiah, when I expect to hear all that is going on in the outer world. We are as happy as the days are long and are having a glorious trip.

Joseph

Notes for Letter 13

This letter is a complete transcript of a letter from Joseph Tubby to his family concerning the events of July 3 when they attempted to navigate up what was then regarded as the upper Beaver River, now called the Shingle Shanty Brook. Tubby's original letter is part of the Joseph Tubby Papers in the Archives of American Art, Smithsonian Institution. The original letter is considerably faded and difficult to transcribe accurately. Fortunately, an earlier transcript exists in the Peggy O'Brien research materials for Artists in the Adirondacks at The Adirondack Experience, The Museum on Blue Lake Mountain. The O'Brien transcript was a great help in deciphering the letter. I have changed nothing except for minor corrections in punctuation and capitalization and the addition of paragraph breaks.

It may seem puzzling that Tubby's letter to his family would be addressed to "Dear Friends." This usage probably stems from the fact that the Tubby family were devout Quakers, who would have customarily addressed each other as "Friends." The "James" and "Josiah" referred to later in the letter are Joseph's brothers. As we shall see, at the time this letter was written, Josiah was already on his way to Lowville, where Puffer would meet him and escort him to camp (see letter 18). Tubby familiarly refers to his longtime friend Jervis McEntee as "Jerv."

As this letter clearly illustrates, the events of July 3 made a deep impression on both young artists. McEntee devoted more pages to July 3 in his trip journal than to any other day. His magazine article "The Lakes of the Wilderness" (1859), repeats the story at length and adds more details, some of which diverge slightly from the account in his journal. All three accounts agree on the central facts of the story. The two sketches by McEntee included with this letter are from "The Lakes of the Wilderness." His sketch of the Shingle Shanty shows Puffer sleeping partly out in the rain, a detail that appeared only in McEntee's magazine article.

All that day, McEntee and Tubby had willingly followed Puffer as he led them up a shallow, winding brook that he assured them would bring them within a short distance of the road to Raquette Lake. The paddling was difficult. It rained hard. The insects were insufferable. When they came to a second fork in the stream, Puffer admitted he had never ascended the stream but was relying on secondhand knowledge. He didn't know which branch to follow and guessed. His guess was wrong. Soon they were stuck in a swamp as daylight started to fade.

Even in this situation, Puffer remained calm and confident that the road had to be nearby to the south. He pointed. The artists had become disoriented and disagreed. Fortunately, they had a compass that showed Puffer was right. As they trudged through the swamp, McEntee started to doubt Puffer again, but Puffer's calm determination drew them forward. They soon made the road and found shelter for the night. McEntee never again doubted Puffer's guiding skills.

Almost exactly twenty years later, in mid-June 1871, H. Perry Smith and seven friends made the same mistake. As with McEntee, the Smith party had to contend with rain, biting insects, and a narrow, shallow stream that, Smith remarked, "didn't remind us of the Hudson." They never reached their intended destination. As a warning to anyone else who might attempt this traverse, Smith noted, "The streams are obstructed and the carries vague or exist only in the imagination of guides."[1]

Five years later, in the summer of 1876, the H. H. Thompson party of three men led by two guides made the same trip up the Beaver, this time with better results.[2] This group successfully navigated the first five or six miles and made camp on a high bank under tamarack trees. During the whole of the next day, they pushed up the *left* fork of the stream, carrying their boats when necessary, passed through a series of small ponds, and finally came to Salmon Lake. Thompson's

1. This trip is described in humorous detail in H. Perry Smith, *Modern Babes in the Woods; Or Summerings in the Wilderness. To Which Is Added a Reliable and Descriptive Guide to the Adirondacks by E. R. Wallace* (Hartford, CT: Columbian Book, 1872), 130–99.

2. See H. H. [Henry Hunn] Thompson, "On the Wilderness Trail," *Forest and Stream* 7, no. 8 (Sept. 28, 1876): 114.

description makes it clear that they were not the only campers to ever ascend the brook as far as Salmon Lake.

This Salmon Lake, distinguished from the one on the Red Horse Chain north of the Beaver River, is in fact somewhat nearer the Carthage–to–Lake Champlain Road and featured a trail that led directly to the road at Brandreth Lake.

Impressions of Beach's Lake, Meeting William Austin

Mr. and Mrs. Philip McEntee, Clinton, Oneida County, New York
Tuesday, July 10, 1851

Dear Uncle Philip and Aunt Lucy,

I trust that during your usual Sunday conversation with Rev. Sawyer following chapel, my old school principal mentioned hearing of my sketching trip to the lakes and mountains of the Adirondacks. Surely my father and mother must have also mentioned it to you.

My friend Joseph Tubby and I are now encamped on the shore of Racket Lake in the very center of that wild region. This is the most beautiful sheet of water I have ever experienced. There is deep forest all around, with lofty mountains rising in the distance. From one spot out on the lake I caught my first glimpse of distant Mount Tahawus, the tallest peak in our fair state.

We arrived here this past Sunday, having spent the previous night in a log shanty at the head of nearby Beach's Lake. I had heard there would be ample scenes for sketching all along Beach's Lake, but Joseph and I agreed the scenery was so ordinary that we decided to move here. I'm glad we did as this lake features more beautiful scenes than we could sketch in a month's time.

While camped for a night at Beach's Lake, we learned that the entire township in which it lies has this spring been purchased by the eminent Dr. Benjamin Brandreth, he of Brandreth's pills. He intends to build himself a wilderness retreat by the lake that he will rename after himself.

A rough road crosses Dr. Brandreth's property connecting it to the remote village of Long Lake. The road itself is "simply a path

through the woods, with an attempt at bridging streams and mo-
rasses with corduroy. It was opened with a view of inducing settlers
to go in and occupy the lands through which it runs. It has had
but little effect in this way, however, and seems practically useless,
as there are often whole years during which it is not traveled by a
single team throughout its entire length. Fishing and hunting parties frequently avail themselves of it in hauling their provisions to
Racket Lake, but the labor of traveling it is more than many care to
undergo."

Puffer, our faithful guide, has a great familiarity with this road as
he was a member of the surveying team that laid out its course in the
summer of '41. The road has not been much maintained, so a wagon
with a team has great difficulty passing across some parts of it.

Dr. Brandreth has already begun repairs to that part of the road
connecting his lake to the outside world. When we arrived at Beach's
Lake, we found a group of six workmen hard at work on the road.
The men are all settlers from the pioneer village at Long Lake. A
man named Austin is the foreman.

The next morning Austin lent us a log dugout canoe so we could
explore the lake. By the time we returned his homemade canoe, we
had decided to move on. When we were eating our dinner at the
workmen's shanty, we learned that a man named Parker was planning
to travel back to his farm at Long Lake that very afternoon. Parker
had a wagon and huge elephant of a horse. He agreed to go back to
fetch our baggage where we had left it and transport it to the place
where the road meets Racket Lake.

After we finished our dinner, Austin gave us some potatoes and
three onions, which we were glad for. He told us he kept a store
of supplies at his farm and that he would be glad to sell us some if
we were ever in need. When Parker arrived with our baggage, we
thanked Austin for his hospitality and proceeded on our way. Because
the road was so uneven, we dared not ride in the wagon but more
comfortably walked the five miles to the shore of Racket Lake.

I will surely have many more stories to tell you when I next visit.
We plan to stay at Racket Lake for two more weeks, then arrange to

climb Blue Mountain, which we can see in the near distance. At the end of the trip we will sketch the famous Indian Pass and hopefully have enough remaining strength to climb Mount Tahawus.

Feel free to show this letter to others in the family and to Rev. Sawyer and his family. Please give my greetings to Gertrude Sawyer should you meet her.

Your nephew,
Jervis

Notes for Letter 14

Philip and Lucy McEntee of Clinton, New York, were Jervis's uncle and aunt. Philip was one of Jervis's father's younger brothers. Jervis probably lived with his aunt and uncle while he attended the Clinton Liberal Institute. During his time at school, the Reverend Thomas Jefferson Sawyer, a Universalist minister, was the school principal and conducted public services at the school's chapel. Since the McEntees lived nearby, it's likely they would have been friendly with Rev. Sawyer. As mentioned in the notes for letter 7, Jervis would marry Gertrude Sawyer in 1854, and Rev. Sawyer would become his father-in-law.

After leaving the Shingle Shanty, the artists came to a roughly Z-shaped lake in the center of Township No. 39 that was traditionally called "Beach's Lake" after an early settler who had built a cabin there. Although that name was still in use when McEntee and Tubby visited, it would soon be changed to "Brandreth Lake" by Dr. Benjamin Brandreth, a successful manufacturer of a popular patent medicine who had purchased all of Township No. 39 in March 1851.

The artists found a snug log cabin on the shore of the lake, where they spent the night. This was probably a cabin Dr. Brandreth had built since he assumed travelers would be passing through his property on the road and wanted to make them feel welcome. Dr. Brandreth was known to welcome the occasional visitor and sometimes lent them a boat or even a horse. The guestbook from the Brandreth visitor's cabin has numerous travelers' entries from 1851 up through 1882.[1]

As noted earlier, much of the artists' trip was along the recently constructed Carthage–to–Lake Champlain Road. The description of the road's poor condition in this letter is a direct quote from McEntee's journal. Although the New York Legislature paid for the creation of the road, it made no specific provision for its upkeep. Instead, the duty and expense of maintaining the road fell to local citizens. It is

---

1. More details about the founding of Brandreth Park can be found in Orlando B. Potter III and Donald Brandreth Potter, *Brandreth: A Band of Cousins Preserves the Oldest Adirondack Family Enclave* (Utica, NY: North Country, 2011).

reasonable that Dr. Brandreth would have wanted to improve the section of the road between his land and Long Lake, which is why the artists encountered a group of men from Long Lake working on the road. The foreman of the road builders was William Austin, and the teamster was Zenas Parker. McEntee will encounter both men again later in the journey.

This letter also introduces two place-names frequently found in the journal. In 1851, the body of water now called "Raquette Lake" was commonly spelled "Racket" or "Rackett." McEntee usually referred to the lake and river flowing out of it as "the Racket." He made the unlikely claim that he caught his first glimpse of Mount Tahawus from Raquette Lake. McEntee, like many others of his time, believed that "Tahawus" was the original Native American name for Mount Marcy. The name does mean "cloud-splitter" in the Seneca language, but it was not the Native American name for Mount Marcy.[2]

2. The name "Tahawus" was first applied to the mountain by Charles Fenno Hoffman in the newspaper article "Scenes at the Source of the Hudson," which was incorporated into his book *Wild Scenes in the Forest and Prairie*, 2 vols. (London: Richard Bentley, 1839–40), 1:177–78. For a good discussion of the misapplication of the name "Tahawus" to Mount Marcy, see Sandra Weber, *Mount Marcy: The High Peak of New York* (Fleischmanns, NY: Purple Mountain Press, 2001), 41–45.

Meeting William Wood, a Night at His Cabin

To Mr. Robert Grosman, Wall St., Kingston, Ulster Co., New York
Tuesday, July 10, 1851

Dear Robert,

When I last saw you in Kingston, I promised to write about my adventures in the wilderness. I regret I have not fulfilled my promise until now. Joe and I have already had many adventures of which I will tell you on my return. Watch for a letter that touches on the highlights of our trip so far that I hope will appear in the Rondout Sunday paper sometime in the near future.

I write you from our camp on the shore of Racket Lake deep in the Adirondack forest. We arrived at the lake this past Sunday and spent our first night in a cabin that is the abode of a man named Wood. "We found his home a very comfortable one, and, though rude, [it] exhibited the unmistakable traces of neatness and industry. The house is built of logs with a bark covered porch in the front, and standing on a gentle elevation about fifty yards from the lake. He has a very good garden entirely free of weeds, and quite a field of rye and potatoes growing."

Wood is a remarkable woodsman. "I wondered when I saw him that a man like him should be able to live in as wild a region. He is an unfortunate cripple, both feet having been frozen so as to render amputation of the legs necessary, and he is compelled to walk on his knees, yet he travels over this wild country for miles in all directions." He and Puffer cooked us an especially delicious supper of venison, potatoes and onions out of our larder. Wood provided us with sweet cherries from his tree and ripe raspberries that grow in abundance 'round his shanty.

OUR SHANTY.

2.3. Jervis McEntee, *Wood's Cabin*, wood engraving by Loomis-Annin from sketch by Jervis McEntee. In McEntee, "The Lakes of the Wilderness," 341. Courtesy of the American Antiquarian Society, Worcester, MA.

We expected Wood to be on the lookout for us when we arrived at this lake as Sylvester had written to him that we were coming and wanted to rent a boat from him. When we reached the lake shore, we built a fire and shot our guns, but Wood did not appear. After an hour we started walking around the lake but soon saw two men coming our way in a boat. We hailed them, supposing it to be Wood. It was not, rather a guide named Arnold from Brown's Tract with Brainard, a sportsman from Albany. They had come in a boat up the Moose River and expected to meet a different party. Arnold rowed us over to Wood's. Wood, having been gone hunting at Blue Mountain, returned to his cabin presently, and after a late supper we all slept on a straw mattress by the fire.

The next morning after a good breakfast on Wood's porch we got a boat from him and rowed across the lake to Constable Point to inspect the camp where we hoped to stay for the following two weeks. We found the camp in good order so after dinner at Wood's we moved our baggage. Arnold needed to return to his hotel, so Brainard asked to join us for a few days while waiting for his friends to arrive. We readily agreed, set up our camp, then rowed out in the lake to see if we could see Mount Tahawus. It was late and the water so rough that we had to be satisfied with a mere glimpse of distant mountains before returning to camp for the night.

The scenes all around this lake are quite wonderful; consequently I fully expect our days here to be mostly occupied with sketching. I thought you might especially enjoy a view of Wood's cabin. Pasted below is the sketch of it I made for you this morning. I will show you the finished drawing when we next meet.

Joe sends you his regards and promises to write you soon.

Your friend,

Jervis

Notes for Letter 15

Robert Grosman, the recipient of this letter, was a Kingston friend of both McEntee and Tubby. He was the son of Rev. John Grosman, former pastor of the Old Dutch Church, the oldest church in Kingston, established in 1659. We know that McEntee corresponded with Grosman during the trip because a surviving letter from Tubby to Grosman sent from the Adirondac Iron Works in August 1851 mentions that McEntee had sent Grosman at least one letter earlier in the trip.[1]

At the time of the trip, Grosman was writing a biography of John Vanderlyn (1776–1852), an internationally recognized neoclassical painter from Kingston. Vanderlyn returned penniless to Kingston in the last years of his life, and Grosman befriended him. Grosman's biography of Vanderlyn was never published, although the manuscript is in the collection at the Senate House Museum in Kingston, which also displays a collection of Vanderlyn's paintings.

William Wood, along with a friend named Mathew Beach, established a wilderness homestead on Raquette Lake around 1837. Beach was the elder of the two, older than seventy when McEntee met him. Wood's first wilderness home was at Thendara, also in the Adirondacks, where he arrived sometime in the early 1830s. While living in Thendara, he suffered severe frostbite, which resulted in amputations of both feet and lower legs. Undeterred, he had special boots made that allowed him to walk on his knees remarkably well.

Beach and Wood initially lived together in a bark shanty on Indian Point, which they gradually transformed into a large log cabin. They cleared ten acres and had a small hayfield and a few cows. They managed to grow some hardy vegetables, including potatoes and turnips, and cultivated a few fruit trees and raspberry bushes. The two men

1. Joseph Tubby to Robert Grosman, [August?] 1851, Joseph Tubby Papers, quoted at length in Levy, *Joseph Tubby*, 10.

eventually had a disagreement and separated around 1845, with Wood relocating across the lake.[2]

Perhaps the only McEntee sketch from this part of the trip in a public art collection is the one he made of Wood's cabin. According to his journal, McEntee worked on this sketch nearly all day on July 18.[3] A copy of McEntee's original sketch appears as figure o.2 after the introduction to this book. The wood engraving of the same view, made from the sketch, is figure 2.3 at the end of letter 15.

Otis Arnold, the man guiding "Brainard," maintained a sportsman's hotel after 1837 in the abandoned Herreshoff Manor at Thendara, New York, also sometimes referred to as Brown's Tract. Thendara is a short distance south of today's village of Old Forge. Arnold charged guests $1.50 a day or $11.00 a week and a separate fee for guiding them.[4]

2. More details about the first two white settlers of Raquette Lake can be found in Tom Thacher, *Fifty Acres of Beach and Wood* (Raquette Lake, NY: Birch Point Press, 2016), 69–80.

3. The original sketch is in the collection of The Adirondack Experience, The Museum on Blue Mountain Lake, and is reproduced in Patricia C. F. Mandel, *Fair Wilderness: American Paintings in the Collection of the Adirondack Museum* (Blue Mountain Lake, NY: Adirondack Museum, 1990), 88.

4. For more on Arnold, see Joseph F. Grady, *The Adirondacks, Fulton Chain—Big Moose Region: The Story of a Wilderness*, 3rd ed. (Utica, NY: North Country, 1972), 88–125.

Quiet Morning on Raquette Lake, His Birthday

To Miss Anna Gertrude Sawyer, c/o Dr. Thomas Jefferson Sawyer,
principal, the Clinton Liberal Institute, Clinton, New York
Monday, July 14, 1851

Dear Gertrude,

Today is my 23rd birthday. I spent the early morning by myself float-ing motionless in a little boat in a bay of beautiful Racket Lake. The air was cool and the water somewhat warmer. Wisps of fog hung over the water, rendering the scene magical. Dark trees all around cast dim shadows on the still water and in the distance out of my sight a solitary loon gave a long mournful cry.

The sky slowly brightened. I looked to the east just as the fiery sun began to show above the trees. When its warm rays reached the water, the fog that hitherto softened the landscape dissipated, revealing the whole of the sparkling lake and the mountains in the distance.

"It was one of the most quiet, peaceful mornings that I ever beheld. The clouds were of that thin hazy appearance which is hardly discernible from the sky and seeming to mingle with it. The motion-less lake gave perfect reflections of objects on shore and was scarcely ruffled in any part, even by the slightest breeze."

As I rowed my boat along, "my thoughts ran home and I formed pictures of how it appeared there. How the quiet Hudson Bay [*sic*] gleams in the sun and the still chestnuts raise their green heads upon the hill. I could not but contrast the noise and tumult of the village to the unbroken silence of this wild spot, and wished in my heart that my friends might be here to look upon the scene of beauty, this

RACQUETTE LAKE.

2.4. Jervis McEntee, *Blue Mountain from Raquette Lake*, wood engraving by Loomis-Annin from sketch by Jervis McEntee. In McEntee, "The Lakes of the Wilderness," 344. Courtesy of the American Antiquarian Society, Worcester, MA.

picture of repose, and have their souls filled with the inexpressible emotions that thrilled me."

Presently I returned to camp intending to bring Joe out to share the scene with me. By the time we had reached the outlet of the lake and set up our sketching stools, though, the wind came up, so we did not get a chance to depict the calm lake as I had experienced it earlier in the morning.

In the far distance we could see the high mountains. Somewhere among them but just out of sight stands Mount Tahawus, tallest of them all. With any luck we will climb to the top of that giant sometime next month. We agreed that the light on the mountains was perfect. Joe and I spent the entire day making sketches of Blue Mountain, the mountain nearest to us. Later next week we plan to relocate our camp to the foot of that mountain and sketch the view of the many lakes that we understand can be seen from its summit.

I made a fair sketch of Racket Lake with Blue Mountain in the background. I cut it out of my sketch book and pasted it here for you. We sketched all day, stopping to fish every hour or so. We caught only three speckled trout between us but were satisfied that they would make us a fine supper.

We returned to camp about 5 o'clock in the evening. A man from Albany named Brainard, who is stopping with us for a few days, already had the supper fire going. I set about cleaning the trout, while Joe mixed up some wheaten cakes using a method he learned from our guide. He lamented that he had not the skill to bake me a birthday cake. I replied that his company in this wild place was birthday gift enough.

I hope you are well. I imagine you walking the green fields and hills around Clinton, singing some sweet song as you go. Please tell my aunt and uncle of this letter when you see them. Give my regards to your father and mother.

Your friend,

Jervis

Notes for Letter 16

In his journal, McEntee says he did nothing special to celebrate his birthday. He and Tubby spent the day sketching at the outlet of Raquette Lake. McEntee specifically notes that he had hoped to sketch the calm lake but was unable to do so because the wind had come up. On several other occasions, he also notes how often the lake was rough and the wind high. My personal experience with canoeing on Raquette Lake confirms this observation. McEntee mentions that Tubby made a sketch of Blue Mountain but does not specify what scene he himself was working on other than to say they sketched the mountains. Figure 2.4 is a copy of the engraving by the firm of Loomis-Annin based on McEntee's sketch of Raquette Lake with Blue Mountain in the background that appeared in "The Lakes of the Wilderness" (1859).

Brainard, the sportsman from Albany who arrived at Raquette Lake on July 9 from Thendara guided by Otis Arnold, expected to find a group of his friends already camped there. Since his friends had not yet arrived, he asked to stay with McEntee and Tubby at the Constable camp. Brainard's friends finally arrived on July 12. The camp had two large lean-tos, so there was adequate room for everyone. Brainard returned to Thendara on the morning of July 16. His friends stayed on and later moved their camp to Blue Mountain Lake (see letters 19 and 20).

In the journal, McEntee gently mocks Brainard because of his obsession with killing a deer, a feat he does not seem to have accomplished. McEntee apparently did not realize that Brainard was typical of the tourists of the time, while he and Tubby were clearly rare exceptions in their outlook. Jervis and Joe had completely adopted their roles as artists. For them, the wilderness was primarily a font of sublime beauty. Thus, they must have thought it an unfortunate blindness for someone to see it only as a place to hunt deer and fish for trout.

Meeting Lewis Elijah Benedict and Mitchel Sabattis

To Miss Augusta McEntee, Clovertop, Rondout, New York
Wednesday, July 16, 1851

Dear Gussie,

This past Saturday as Joe and I were rowing down the lake towards the outlet where we planned to spend the day sketching and fishing, as has been our habit on most days since arriving at Racket Lake, we heard gunshots from nearby. As this is the customary way in these parts to summon help or attract attention, we landed our boat at the end of a peninsula where one of the two men who live here has his cabin. His name is Beach. He has been here for about twenty years. He has a tight cabin and about ten acres of cleared land where he grows some hardy vegetables. He also keeps a few cows. He is tall and has a shaggy gray beard, being perhaps seventy years old.

A skiff was pulled up along the shore near Beach's cabin and beside it a birch-bark Indian canoe. Before we could get out of our boat, Beach appeared and greeted us. He told us that a party of three from Albany had just arrived and were trying to find a friend who was supposed to have come in a few days earlier. We surmised immediately that they were seeking our new friend Brainard. We advised Beach as much and told him that Brainard was at our camp spending his day relaxing and fishing from shore.

We had started up the path to Beach's cabin when we were met by another old man with the unmistakable features of a full-blooded Indian. Beach introduced him as Elijah and claimed that he was the first person in the entire region to be able to make something of a living by guiding visitors. Elijah smiled and nodded at this. Elijah

shook hands with us both and asked if we possibly had enough
room at our camp to accommodate his party. We said that we did
and would be glad of the company. We told him that Brainard was
already with us and was waiting for his brother and his friends
to arrive.

At Beach's cabin we met the three men from Albany. Brainard's
brother was not with them as he had fallen ill the day before the
other three departed the capital city. To my surprise and delight their
second guide was none other than Headley's Indian guide Mitchel,
on whom Headley has heaped so much praise. Mitchel is much
younger than I expected, being perhaps no more than twenty-five
years old. He is short of stature, with the quiet grace of a man totally
at home in the wilderness. Almost at once he and Elijah embarked
with their party, bound for our camp to rendezvous with Brainard.

When we returned to camp in the early afternoon, we found
Elijah there alone as Brainard and the rest had gone off fishing with
Mitchel. Elijah told us that he lived at Indian Lake with his niece and
his 105-year-old father, Sabael, who had moved to the Adirondacks
just after the War for Independence. He especially emphasized how
hard and cold the winters get here and how once while he was out
on snowshoes checking his traps, he came upon the body of another
trapper who had frozen to death in the woods. He talked freely with
us until the others came back and he had to go cook them supper.

During our talk I asked Elijah where he got his canoe. For a moment he looked surprised and then proudly told me that he had made
it. He said that his people had made bark canoes for centuries. I asked
him if he would allow me to try to paddle it. He laughed and said
I could try, but he would not promise I could do it. Early the next
morning he showed me how to use his paddle. I managed a short voy-
age on my own. What a magnificent craft it proved to be, although
requiring a great deal of attention to prevent a capsize.

It was quite windy all day today, so I stayed in camp. Despite the
poor weather Brainard left early this morning to return to Brown's
Tract, thirty miles distant. The others went out fishing but got
caught in a sudden thunderstorm and soon returned soaked to the

skin. Their early return provided me with an opportunity to make sketches of Elijah and Mitchel. My sketch of Elijah turned out quite well. The one I hastily made of Mitchel, unfortunately, is not a very good likeness.

I always enjoy getting letters from you. Please write again soon with lots of news from home. I trust you will share this letter with family and friends so they can know we are well and thoroughly enjoying our adventure.

Affectionately, your brother,
Jervis

Notes for Letter 17

Lewis Elijah Benedict, also just called "Elijah" or "Lige," was Abenaki, son of Sabael, the first settler at Indian Lake. Lewis Elijah may well have a valid claim to being the first professional Adirondack guide. In 1826, he guided David Henderson to a large deposit of iron ore in a place that would later become the Adirondac Iron Works. He also guided for Professor Farrand Benedict during many of the professor's trips to the Adirondacks beginning in 1835. It is said that Elijah adopted Benedict's last name as his own because of his admiration of the professor. He also guided for Ebenezer Emmons's geological survey of 1836–40. An excellent first-person account of his skill as a guide can be found in newspaper articles in 1855 by Henry J. Raymond, the first editor of the *New York Times*. Lewis Elijah Benedict died in 1866.

One of the first things McEntee observed about Lewis Elijah was that he was old. That observation appears to have been correct. When Rev. John Todd visited Lewis Elijah and his father, Sabael, at their home on Indian Lake in 1852, he learned that Lewis Elijah was about sixty years old, making his birth date around 1792.[1]

Even though Lewis Elijah Benedict was arguably the most important guide working in the Central Adirondacks at the time, McEntee appears not to have been interested in learning much about him. Indeed, McEntee may not even have known his whole name as he never refers to Lewis Elijah by any other name except "Elijah." One way we can be certain that the Native American guide he met was actually Lewis Elijah Benedict is that McEntee noted this guide was accompanied by a dog named Whitefoot, which Rev. Todd noted was the name of Lewis Elijah's favorite dog when he met him the next summer. It was surely the same dog, even though McEntee transliterated its name as "Wampasut" and Rev. Todd as "Wam-pa-ye-tah."

Likewise, McEntee does not tell us much about Mitchel Sabattis and never refers to him except by his first name. He noted on first

---

1. See John Todd, DD, *Summer Gleanings: Or, Sketches and Incidents of a Pastor's Vacation* (Northampton, MA: Hopkins, Bridgman, 1852), 261–66.

meeting Sabattis that he was surprised that Mitchel was only around twenty-five years old. In fact, in July 1851 Sabattis would have been twenty-seven. As McEntee also correctly notes, in 1846–47 Mitchel guided for Joel T. Headley, who praised his skill as a guide in his popular book *The Adirondack; Or, Life in the Woods* (1849).

Mitchel Sabattis was born in 1823 in Parishville, St. Lawrence County, New York. He was also Abenaki. Both he and Lewis Elijah were sometimes referred to as "St. Francis Indians" because their ancestral Abenaki band, originally from Norridgewock, Maine, had relocated to Sainte-Françoise, Québec, in the early eighteenth century to escape attacks by English settlers. At the age of seven, Mitchel began to accompany his father, Captain Peter Sabattis, on hunting expeditions. At eleven, he became one of the earliest settlers of Long Lake, moving there with his father in 1834. His began guiding sportsmen in 1843, when he was nineteen. In 1844, he married a neighbor, Elizabeth A. Dornburgh, called "Betsy." According to many of the early writers, Sabattis was the greatest of the old-time Adirondack guides. His feats in the forest were legendary, and, although small in stature, he possessed great physical strength. When not guiding, he farmed land near Newcomb. After their marriage, Mitchel and Betsy built a sportsman's hotel along Long Lake at the location of today's Paddler's Rest motel. Betsy Sabattis ran the hotel until 1878, while Mitchel continued guiding. Mitchel had a stroke in 1886, which ended his guiding career. He was an important source for much of what is known of Abenaki place-names in the Adirondacks. He told Dyneley Prince that the Abenaki name for Mount Marcy was "Wah-um-de-neg," meaning "It Is Always White," the same name the Abenaki used for the mountains in New Hampshire.[2] Mitchel Sabattis died at Long Lake on April 16, 1906, at the age of eighty-three.[3]

2. See J. Dyneley Prince, "Some Forgotten Indian Place-Names in the Adirondacks," *Journal of American Folk-Lore*, Apr. 1900, 123–28.

3. For more on the life of Mitchel Sabattis, see Melissa Otis, *Rural Indigenousness: A History of Iroquoian and Algonquian Peoples of the Adirondacks* (Syracuse, NY: Syracuse Univ. Press, 2018), 121–29.

In his journal, McEntee says he made a sketch of Lewis Elijah Benedict on July 16 and that it was a good likeness. That sketch, as well as the one he made of Mitchel Sabattis on July 19, have been lost. This is especially unfortunate in the case of Lewis Elijah because there are no existing portraits of him. Because Mitchel Sabattis was still alive when photographers reached the central Adirondacks, there are numerous good photographs of him as an older man.

A Trip to Long Lake for Supplies and Boot Repair

To Mr. & Mrs. James S. McEntee, Clovertop, Rondout, New York
Tuesday, July 22, 1851

Dear Father, dear Mother,

Puffer returned to camp this past Sunday, having gone back to Lowville to pick up supplies and bring in his hay. You will be glad to learn that Joe's brother Josiah was safely with Puffer and full of enthusiasm for our adventures. He brought the bundle of things you sent, including the fine new hat and a new pair of unmentionables. To my great dismay he did not have the new boots I ordered. Puffer says he picked them up at the shoemaker's and put them in Josiah's pack, but they must have been stolen before they left Lowville. That explanation appears somewhat suspect to me.

Even though we had just received some new provisions, we were running out of flour and sugar. Puffer offered to go to Austin's farm at Long Lake to see if he could get those necessities there. When we met Austin at Beach's Lake a few weeks ago, he had mentioned that he kept a supply of staples and offered to provision us if we had the need. My boots were in terrible condition. I feared that without significant repair I would soon be walking through the woods bare-footed. In hope that there might be a shoemaker at Long Lake, I decided to accompany Puffer.

Early Monday morning we rowed to the outlet where the road comes closest to the lake. Judge Seger and some friends are camped there. They greeted us warmly, for Puffer had given them a deer he shot the day before. We did not tarry long, for it is a sixteen-mile walk from Racket Lake to Austin's. As we hurried along, we chanced

on a crew of men who were busy building piers and dams so that logs
could be floated down the Racket River all the way to the St. Lawrence. About 3 o'clock we emerged from the forest at the south end
of Long Lake, where Austin had cleared about fifty acres. His farm
is well kept with strong fences around pastures that hold a goodly
number of cattle. By all appearances Austin is able to make his living
farming, not from the forest, as we were to presently learn is not the
case with many of his neighbors.

Austin was pleased to see us and invited us to sit down to a dinner
of warm bread with butter and fresh milk. "Mrs. Austin keeps such
a tidy house that it is easy to forget we are so far back in the forest."
Austin lent us his boat so we could row about two miles across the
lake to Robinson's. Mr. R has shoemaking tools, but his wife told us
he was not home because he had gone further down the lake to hunt
a bear. We waited for an hour, but when he did not appear, we rowed
back to Austin's. After a good supper we slept in a comfortable bed
for the first time in six weeks.

After breakfast the next morning we rowed back to Robinson's.
He was expecting us and immediately "set to work on my boots while
talking nonstop and eating innumerable biscuits." He did a right
credible job. We started back for Austin's about noon. Unfortunately,
a gale was blowing against us and we did not reach our destination
until well after dinnertime. To our great delight Mrs. Austin had
saved us some ham and biscuits. We bought flour, molasses and sugar
and loaded these supplies into Puffer's commodious knapsack.

We arrived back at Racket Lake to find the Judge and his friends
were busy preparing a venison supper. We ate with them, then rowed
back across the lake to camp in the twilight. Joe and Josiah were
glad to see us safely returned. With a shameful look on his face, Joe
admitted that earlier in the day he had tried to use my sketching
umbrella as a boat sail but the wind was so strong it snatched it from
his hands and straightaway it sank in the lake. We resolved to try to
find it in the morning.

Although I was mighty tired, I decided to sit by the firelight and
write to you before taking to bed as we will break camp tomorrow

morning and relocate to the foot of Blue Mountain, being about fourteen miles distant by water. Thank you for your long letter with news from home and for the things you sent with Josiah. I will write again as soon as I can.

Your obedient son,
Jervis

Notes for Letter 18

Puffer left Raquette Lake for Lowville on July 11 to obtain additional supplies. On the way he presumably retrieved the boats they had left along the Shingle Shanty Brook. When he returned on July 20, he was accompanied by Josiah Tubby, Joe's younger brother. I was initially confused about the identity of the person who joined the artists. The typescript of McEntee's journal entry for July 11 says Puffer will be bringing in "Josiah Tully" to join them. I have carefully examined the handwritten journal and concluded that "Tully" is a transcription error.

McEntee continued to be troubled by his poor choice of boots. We learned in the journal excerpt at the end of part one that by July 2, only three weeks into the trip, his bootheels had loosened to the point that he spent a morning trying to reattach them using pieces of lathe nails he broke in two and whittled to a point. McEntee's makeshift boot repair held up for only a few weeks.

When Puffer headed back to town on July 11, McEntee instructed Puffer to bring him a sturdy pair of new boots when he returned to camp. For reasons that were never clear, the new boots did not make it back to Raquette Lake, even though Puffer brought new pairs for himself and Joe Tubby. In typical style, McEntee quickly moved on to finding a solution rather than spending time placing blame. He imagined he might be able buy new boots at Long Lake or at least find someone with the necessary tools to make repairs. As luck would have it, a Long Lake settler named Robinson had the necessary shoemaking tools to complete temporary repairs.

McEntee and Puffer met four men from Martinsburgh camped along the road near Raquette Lake, including "Judge S." In his later letter to the *Lowville Northern Journal*, McEntee revealed this was Judge Francis Seger, whom he described as a "prince of good fellows." Seger had been elected the first county court judge for Lewis County in 1847 and served in that position until 1856. He had previously been a member of the state legislature, where he introduced the bill that led to the creation of the Black River Canal.[1]

1. See Hough, *History of Lewis County, New York*, 131.

William Austin and his wife, Lois, were early settlers of Long Lake, having moved there from Vermont around 1840. C. W. Webber, who visited the Austin home two years before McEntee and Tubby made their trip, in 1849, described William as a "rather tall, large and very muscular man, quiet in his manners and not much possessed of the gift of gab." McEntee was full of praise for the industry and intelligence of Mrs. Austin. Webber described Lois Austin as "a short, stout, good natured kind of body, about his age and equally quiet."[2] William and Lois Austin raised three children at their farm on Long Lake before moving to nearby Newcomb.

William Austin built "carry boats," possibly modeled on Higby's light boats described earlier. Austin was documented as having met Higby during the Constable family camping trip in 1850.[3]

2. The quotes from Webber probably come from C. W. [Charles Wilkins] Webber, "Original Letters from a Sporting Naturalist," *Spirit of the Times*, Nov. 24, 1849, but their provenance is unclear in the source where I found them: "Long Lake Wesleyan Church: History," updated Apr. 24, 2020, https://llwesleyan.com/index.php/history-of-llwc/. The article from *Spirit of the Times* is mentioned in Thacher, *Fifty Acres*, 72.

3. Austin's boats are described in Sulavik, *The Adirondack Guideboat*, 44–45.

Impressions of Blue Mountain (Ragged) Lake

To Miss Julia McEntee, c/o Mr. Charles McEntee,
Rondout, New York
Thursday, July 24, 1851

Dear Cousin Julia,

Joe, Josiah and I arrived at the foot of Blue Mountain at sunset yesterday. After we left our comfortable camp at Racket Lake, we stopped at Wood's to pay him for our use of his boat for the last three weeks and to arrange for him to retrieve it from our camp at Blue Mountain, for we will not return but rather will carry our baggage overland from here to Long Lake.

To reach Blue Mountain from Racket Lake we ascended a stream that stretches all the way to Ragged Lake, the beautiful water that laps at the foot of the mountain. We rowed up this stream a few miles until we reached some narrows. There we unloaded and carried our supplies around while Puffer pulled the empty boat upstream for about one hundred rods. Above the narrows, the stream is so shallow that we were obliged in several places to climb out and push the boat along until we reached a small lake. Across that lake was another shallow inlet and then a second lake much like the first. On the far side of the second lake, we pushed and pulled the loaded boat up a small rapid. At long last we entered upon the waters of Ragged Lake, our destination for the day.

"It was near sunset when we came into the lake, and the tremendous mountain rising three thousand feet from the lake gave us an imposing view with its base in shadow and its summit glowing in the red sunlight." We did not tarry to observe the scenery, for all four of

RAGGED LAKE.

2.5. Jervis McEntee, *Ragged Lake*, wood engraving by Loomis-Annin from sketch by Jervis McEntee. In McEntee, "The Lakes of the Wilderness," 345. Courtesy of the American Antiquarian Society, Worcester, MA.

us were chilled and hungry. I fired my gun. A return report answered from across the waters. Looking in that direction we saw smoke rising near a long sand beach. We hurried ashore there. Friends we met at Racket Lake had already established themselves near the beach, so we moved off a short way to other level ground. While Joe, Josiah and I set up the tent, Puffer cooked supper. Settled at last, we christened our new home "Camp Church" in honor of Mr. Church, the artist.

We woke this morning to the sound of a steady rain on the canvas. About noon it cleared off. We rowed out to a wooded island to take in the sublime scene. Joe and I sketched for a few hours while Josiah and Puffer occupied themselves by catching several fat trout that we later had for supper. My sketch pleased me much so I wanted to share it with you.

After darkness fell, Puffer and I went floating for deer, but although we searched all the likeliest places, we never saw a one. "It is only at night on these lone lakes that I can realize we are so far in the forest. The dark waters and the sounding woods that echo back the scream of the loon have an effect of wildness and loneliness that the daytime robs them of. As we glided noiselessly along the shadowy banks our light shone down in the clear water upon the rocks making them appear so near that it seemed as though the boat must touch them. Occasionally as we would turn a point the fire from our camp gleaned out upon the gloom from the foot of the mountain that rose solemnly up into the night from the head of the lake casting a dark reflection nearly halfway across occasionally rippled with twinkling lights as a flock of ducks rose from beneath his shadow or the night breeze swept lightly over it."

Even though it has been a full six weeks since we entered the wilderness, we "have no inclination to go home, not having as yet grown weary of wood life. We shall look rather ferocious when we return, for our beards are unshorn and will be until we get back again, for we have no razor with us."

When Joe's brother Josiah arrived a few days ago he brought along a bundle of letters, including your welcome missive. Please write again to let me know if you care for the sketch I have included with this letter. We can receive letters at the post office at the Adirondac Iron Works, where we will be until the middle of next month.

Affectionately, your cousin,
Jervis

Notes for Letter 19

Blue Mountain and the chain of lakes stretching to Raquette Lake were known by a confusing array of names during the nineteenth century. The names used were a mix of traditional local names and the names conferred by early surveyors, especially Professor Ebenezer Emmons, director of the state's geological survey for the northern division of New York State. The name "Blue Mountain" arose from local usage. It appeared in written accounts as early as 1847. Other early names were "Mount Emmons" and "Mount Clinch." By the time McEntee arrived at this mountain in 1851, the name "Blue Mountain" was the most common for it.

Similarly, the name of the lake fluctuated over time. It appears that the name "Blue Mountain" was applied to the lake before it was applied to the mountain. It first appeared on the map drawn by J. L. Harris in 1843. An article in the *Sabbath Recorder* for July 28, 1853, listed the variety of names for the lake as "Blue Mountain," "Ragged," "Eckford," "Clinch," "Emmons," "Tallo," and "Tallow." The article claimed the name "Tallow Lake" was given by hunters to refer to the fatness of the deer around the lake. When McEntee visited in 1851, "Ragged Lake" was probably the favorite local designation, so that is how he refers to it in his journal.

McEntee did not trouble to learn the name of the river and chain of lakes that ascended from Raquette Lake. Professor Emmons, during his survey of the area in 1840, collectively referred to the three lakes as the "Eckford Chain of Lakes" in honor of Henry Eckford, a renowned shipbuilder and father-in-law of James E. DeKay, the zoologist for the survey. Emmons named the waterway that connects the chain to Raquette Lake the "Marion River," after Marion Bedell, the wife of Henry Eckford.[1]

---

1. The information regarding the early history and naming of the Blue Mountain area relies on the detailed article by John Sasso, "Historical Profile—Blue Mountain: Beyond the Fire Tower," History and Legends of the Adirondacks, Facebook group, Nov. 27, 2017, https://www.facebook.com/groups/adirondackhistory/.

The quotation near the end of this letter about McEntee and Tubby having grown beards is from the article in the *Lowville Northern Journal* published on August 27, 1851.[2] This suggests that prior to the trip they were clean-shaven. Photographs taken later in their lives, such as those on the title page of this book, show both artists with long, full beards, so perhaps they first adopted this appearance during their sketching trip.

2. McEntee, "'Camp Church,' Ragged Lake, July 24, 1851."

Climbing Blue Mountain

To Nathaniel B. Sylvester, Esq., N. State St., Lowville, New York
Friday, July 25, 1851

Dear friend Sylvester,

We climbed to the top of Blue Mountain this day. Since you are well
acquainted with the Constable family, I thought you might be interested in my report of what we saw and didn't see. Accordingly, having
already had my supper thanks to Puffer, I will describe the climb to
you as best I can.

It was raining lightly when we awoke but cleared off about 10
o'clock, at which time a doctor from the Albany party camping near
us appeared and asked whether we wanted to accompany him up the
mountain. The weather looked unsettled to me, but since the others
were eager to go, I relented.

Our party comprised Joe, his brother Josiah, me, and the doctor,
guided by the Indian Elijah, who was accompanied by his little dog,
Wampasut. We started up from a bay on the east side of the lake.
The way was very abrupt and the footing difficult. In a short time,
we reached the first ridge, where we paused to catch our breath and
view the summit still high above us. The doctor had been lagging
and complained of feeling unwell. He said he wished to abandon
the enterprise. "The truth of the matter was I suspect that he was
unequal to the task and if he had known its difficulties would not
have started."

The rest of us had no intention of turning back. Soon we were
again climbing upwards, often over loose rocks covered in wet moss.
Presently we struck a blazed line that we followed to the top. Before we reached the summit, it began to rain hard and we were soon

wet to the skin. The doctor was by this time quite miserable. Elijah built us a fire with great difficulty. We huddled around it and tried to cheer the doctor by joking. One of us chanced to observe that he looked a bit like a wet rooster. Despite our best efforts he continued to mourn his decision to suggest the climb.

Admittedly, I regretted exceedingly that we had not come on a clear day. When the rain abated somewhat, Elijah led us to a place where the trees had been cut down. He said from there we could get a view of the lake, but because of the thick mist we only caught occasional glimpses of "two or three lakes and three clearings having houses and barns, oases in this unknown land." We waited a long time at the opening, but the mist grew thicker. I particularly wanted to see the high Adirondacks from our vantage. Elijah led me around to the northeastern side of the summit, where there is another opening, but sadly the mountains were barely visible through the gloom.

Before we started down, Elijah took us to an old dead pine and pointed to marks deeply cut into one side. On close observation we could make out a neat row of initials that Elijah told us were those of the Constable party, including four ladies, who had climbed the mountain almost exactly a year ago. "I presume these are the only ladies whose feet ever trod these lofty heights and they certainly deserve great praise for their courage and hardihood in undertaking and accomplishing so difficult a feat."

Elijah was not their guide, but he later met Higbie, who had guided them. Higbie told Elijah that he rowed the party up from Racket Lake during the day. They started their climb just after 5 o'clock in the afternoon and encamped on the summit. Elijah then led us along a surveyor's line a short distance to a hut made of sticks and moss, with the remains of a fire in front of it. Here's where they must have spent the night with the eternal stars above them.

Our inspection of the summit concluded, we started down in haste. We hoped to arrive back at camp before the rain returned, but it met us halfway. It took us about an hour and ten minutes to descend. We went down by a different route that brought us to within forty rods of our camp. Puffer had supper ready when we arrived.

Tomorrow we will relocate to Austin's farm at Long Lake, carrying our baggage overland. After spending a few days sketching there, we will proceed to the Iron Works, where we will stay long enough to sketch the Indian Pass, as Cole did only a few years past, and climb Mount Tahawus. You can write me there with any news you might have.

>With kindest regards,
>   Your friend,
>   Jervis McEntee

Notes for Letter 20

Lewis Elijah Benedict was probably more familiar with Blue Mountain than anyone else alive in 1851. Although others likely climbed the mountain before he did, Lewis Elijah made the first recorded climb in 1840. That summer he guided Professor Ebenezer Emmons's geological survey crew from Lake Pleasant at today's Speculator to Raquette Lake by way of Indian Lake and Blue Mountain. When the party reached a marsh, now Lake Durant, near the base of Blue Mountain, Lewis Elijah became unsure of the proper route forward. Embarrassed, he exclaimed to Emmons, "It would do for a white man to be lost, but never do for an Indian." He told them to wait a while, then left the group. Four hours later he returned to report seeing Raquette Lake and Long Lake from the summit of Blue Mountain and now knew the way. This event was included in Emmons's subsequent published report to the state legislature.[1]

McEntee and friends climbed one of the steeper slopes of Blue Mountain. There was no established trail for much of the way, but nearer the summit they found a blazed trail. There is no record of who marked out that trail or why. At the summit, Lewis Elijah took the group to two separate lookouts from which the trees had been cleared. Again, there is no record of who cut down the trees or why. One possibility is suggested by the presence of a surveyor's line on the summit. The outside borders of Township No. 19 of the Totten and Crossfield Purchase, where Blue Mountain is located, were first surveyed by Ebenezer Jessup and Israel Thompson in 1772.[2] It seems reasonable that Blue Mountain, given its elevation, might have served one or more subsequent surveys, resulting in the cutting of a survey line and lookouts. That the trees had not grown back by 1851 suggests that there had been recent surveying activity. The record of this later survey, if there was one, has not been found.

1. See Sasso, "Historical Profile—Blue Mountain."
2. The early observations and surveys of Blue Mountain are detailed in Sasso, "Historical Profile—Blue Mountain."

During the Constable family camping trip to Raquette Lake in July 1850, their guide, William Higby, led a group on a climb of Blue Mountain. McEntee says he saw the initials of four ladies carved in a tree at the summit of the mountain, but credible accounts of the Constable trip show there was a total of seven women and six men in the Constable party. It is not recorded how many of them climbed Blue Mountain. The women were Anna Constable, Matilda and Annie McVickar, Cornelia Lent, Jane and Mary Major, and Sarah Richards.[3] Although other women may have made the climb at some earlier date, the women of the Constable party are the first on record to have done so. Apparently, they enjoyed the climb so much that some of them returned in the late summer of 1851, only to be rewarded with an intense thunderstorm while camped overnight on the summit.

3. See Pilcher, *The Constables*, 64.

A Tiresome Hike to Long Lake

To Calvert Vaux, c/o Downing & Vaux,
Architects, Newburgh, New York
Sunday, July 27, 1851

Dear friend Calvert,

I received a letter from my sister Mary recently that conveyed your wish to hear more about our sketching trip directly from me. I am most happy to oblige.

I woke this sabbath day in a feather bed in an upstairs room at Austin's farmhouse that I share with the three others in our party: Joe and Josiah Tubby, brothers from Rondout, and our trusty guide, Puffer. Austin reserves this large room for such travelers that might happen this way and he claims that it is used often enough to afford him a nice income to supplement his farming. His house and farm are very well kept and by far the most prosperous one here. We plan to remain until the end of the month to do some sketching and build up our strength.

Just yesterday we undertook a most strenuous relocation from our tent camp at the foot of Blue Mountain to this place overlooking Long Lake. Because we had to carry our baggage for six miles over rough country, we left everything behind that we did not absolutely need. We made a gift of heavy parcels of flour, corn meal and molasses to a party of men from Albany who were remaining behind at Blue Mountain for a few more days.

We started about noon by rowing across the lake to the trail. By prior arrangement we left the boat there for the man who lent it to us to pick up later. Our packs "consisted of the whole camp equipage besides the tent, our knapsacks and sketching boxes. We had all we could travel under and the day being warm and the path rough and hilly made it very laborious." Puffer carried the heaviest pack with our tent, frying pan, pots, dishes, silverware, etc., as well as gunpowder, shot and his rifle and fishing rod. The three of us carried knapsacks containing our clothes, blankets and other personal belongings. Each of us carried our gun and a fishing rod in a free hand. At the crest of one tall hill, I briefly became so dizzy and partly blind from the weight on my back that I had to stop for a moment until the spell passed.

Our way was difficult, with hills and marshy places, but it was so beautiful that I regretted we had not the time to stop for a sketch. Imagine, if you can, an unbroken forest all around, winding small streams and green openings dotted with wildflowers and grasses. Twice we passed ponds that appeared as they probably have since the time of Adam. As hard as our way proved to be, it was so wild and untouched that I would gladly return to paint it.

At last, we came to the shore of South Pond and threw off our packs. We had been told that there would be a boat there, but there was none. There is no path around this pond and the terrain is quite steep and rough. Puffer opined that someone must have used the boat recently, so he would have to go fetch it from the far side. He disappeared into the thicket and was gone for an hour. We were starting to despair when we caught sight of him rowing a boat towards us.

"We were greatly rejoiced and made the solitudes ring with our shouts. As he got nearer to us, we began to have misgivings about her capacity for carrying all our luggage she was so small and besides was very badly furnished the oars resembling a pudding stick and a baker's peel." Although we doubted her capacity, we loaded the boat. When we were all crowded in, I took the oars and we pushed off. Puffer bailed and I rowed as best I could, and in this fashion we managed to keep her afloat until we reached the far shore.

Taking up our packs again, we ascended a hill and came to a large clearing with an untenanted house and good barn. Puffer lightened his pack considerably by leaving the tent there, planning to retrieve it on the morrow. From the clearing we passed down a rough lane and soon came to the bridge over the outlet of South Pond on the main road leading to Austin's. There we met by chance Mr. Hough, who congratulated us for carrying so well. We arrived at Austin's farm at 7 in the evening and had a good supper before retiring.

I will tell you more of our story when I next see you in the fall. For now, I remain,

Your friend,

Jervis

Notes for Letter 21

Calvert Vaux (1824–95), the recipient of this letter, was an architect who moved from London to Newburgh, New York, in 1850 to work with Andrew Jackson Downing (1815–52), generally credited with being America's first landscape architect. In 1851, the two formed a professional partnership, Downing & Vaux, Architects. Together they designed the grounds surrounding the US Capitol and the Smithsonian Institution. Downing was killed in a steamboat accident in 1852. Vaux continued to do significant landscape work, primarily in association with Frederick Law Olmsted, including the design of Central Park in New York City, Prospect Park in Brooklyn, as well as city parks in Chicago, Buffalo, and many other cities.

Vaux was a talented architect of the neo-Gothic style. He designed a studio for Jervis McEntee in 1853 that was built on part of the McEntee farm in Rondout. In 1872, he worked with Frederic Church to design Church's magnificent home, Olana, overlooking the Hudson River.

According to Lowell Thing, Jervis McEntee may have been introduced to Calvert Vaux in 1850 at the home of A. J. Downing.[1] Downing frequently held gatherings of like-minded horticulturists, architects, and some of the painters of the Hudson River School. It was also at one of Downing's parties that Vaux met then horticulturist and gentleman farmer Frederick Law Olmsted.

Calvert Vaux may have also first met Jervis's next-youngest sister, Mary S. McEntee (1830–92), at one of Downing's gatherings. They were married in 1854. After that, Vaux became an integral part of the McEntee family. Even after Calvert and Mary moved to New York City, they and their four children would spend the holidays at the McEntee home in Rondout.

The difficult hike to Long Lake undertaken by McEntee's party followed an established hunter's trail for about six miles. They left Blue Mountain Lake at the place where a small stream enters, flowing

---

1. Thing, *The Street That Built a City*, 50.

from Minnow Pond. Following the stream to the pond, they proceeded along the south shore to the east end of Minnow Pond, where the path turned north toward Mud Pond on a track roughly parallel to today's Route 28N. Passing the east end of Mud Pond, they crossed a neck of land to the south shore of South Pond. It was a hot day. At one point, McEntee almost fainted from the exertion.

Puffer retrieved a leaky boat with two makeshift oars from the far shore of South Pond. McEntee observes in his journal that the oars resembled a "pudding stick and a baker's peel." A pudding stick has a long shaft that is slightly thicker at one end and is used to stir mush or Indian pudding over a fire. A baker's peel is a stick with a flat shovel on one end, now commonly used to remove pizza from an oven. South Pond is about a mile long. Once across the pond, they followed the outlet stream about half a mile farther to the road to Long Lake and their destination, Austin's farm.

Although McEntee complained about how hard the day was for him, he recorded that as they approached Long Lake, a local man complimented them on how well they carried their gear. Clearly, McEntee wanted to memorialize the fact that they were starting to be noticed as competent woodsmen. The man they encountered was probably Amos Hough, another of the early settlers of Long Lake. It's possible they had already met Hough at Mathew Beach's cabin on Raquette Lake because by 1849 the ageing Beach had invited Hough to live with him and in return for his help gave him the deed to his property while retaining a life use.[2] Beach died in 1862.

2. Thacher, *Fifty Acres*, 80.

Thoughts Concerning the Wilderness Landscape

*To Mr. Frederic E. Church, the American
Art-Union Bldg., New York, New York
Wednesday, July 30, 1851*

Dear Mr. Church,

In keeping with my promise to you, here is a report of the progress
of our sketching trip. We are several days at Long Lake, so called
because the lake is actually a wide part of the Racket River, running
for about fourteen miles, hemmed in by low hills on both sides. The
community consists of but ten or twelve families. In large part these
families make their living from the surrounding forest, not farming.
The soil in most places is very poor and the growing season short.
As a consequence, many former clearings are grown up in trees, with
farm buildings falling into ruin.

    We are staying in the spare room of the Austin family home. It
is located at the head of the lake near where the river enters. Unlike
his neighbors' places, Austin's farm appears quite prosperous. He has
large, cleared fields and a good barn where he keeps a small herd of
cattle, some pigs and some horses.

    We arrived here this past Saturday evening after a fatiguing
six-mile walk over rough ground from our camp at the foot of Blue
Mountain. We called our modest tent camp there "Camp Church"
in your honor, for it was during my discussions with you this past
winter that you suggested I might want to make this sketching trip.
I recall as well how you told me that Thomas Cole relished the wild
scenery of the Adirondacks. You mentioned that on his last trip in
1846 he spent several days sketching here at Long Lake. The scenery

is quite fine indeed and it is a pity that death took Cole before he could make finished paintings from all his sketches.

In the early days of my apprenticeship with you we spent some hours discussing the famous essay Cole wrote on the distinctive characteristics of American scenery. His bold statement that the most distinctive, and perhaps the most impressive, characteristic of American scenery is its wildness has been often in my mind during this trip. To this point I have made sketches of lakes, rivers, forest, mountains and sky but until now I had not encountered a waterfall worth taking time to sketch.

Not far from Austin's, near where the river empties into the lake it passes over a falls about twenty feet high. The location is very picturesque, with a sawmill near the falls. I was attracted especially by a view of some rocks where the water collides and pours over in a great rush. Joe agreed that it was just the waterfall scene we were seeking. We did not set to work immediately because Austin had told us of another mill about three miles along the road in the other direction, and we walked there to see if the scene was better. We were disappointed and so early on Monday we returned to the first falls, set up our stools and began our sketches.

We sketched for most of the day on Monday, except when some passing showers forced us to take shelter in the mill. We returned yesterday and stayed all day. At one point we heard a party passing by on the road to Racket Lake, but we did go out to meet them. Today was a fine day without rain; accordingly we were able to nearly complete our sketches before returning to Austin's for a trout supper. With any luck we will finish our waterfall sketches tomorrow. I will make you a small study of the scene and enclose it with this letter for your perusal.

As I was sketching these past days, my mind returned again and again to the high regard Cole held for waterfalls. If I recall correctly, he felt every landscape to be defective without water and favored waterfalls especially because they give voice to the landscape. I cannot help but agree that they are beautiful for that reason and because they convey the "apparently incongruous idea of fixedness and

FALLS OF THE RACQUETTE

2.6. Jervis McEntee, *Falls of the Raquette River*, wood engraving by Loomis-Annin from sketch by Jervis McEntee. In McEntee, "The Lakes of the Wilderness," 346. Courtesy of the American Antiquarian Society, Worcester, MA.

motion—a single existence in which we perceive unceasing change and everlasting duration."

We will leave this place on Friday and relocate to the Iron Works, where we plan to sketch the famous Indian Pass. A man from here has agreed to take our baggage there in his wagon, so the journey should be a pleasant one.

With kindest regards,

Jervis

Notes for Letter 22

Much of this letter concerns the influence of Thomas Cole on McEntee's art. Cole was born in England in 1801. In 1818 at the age of seventeen, he immigrated to the United States with his family. He initially worked in his father's wallpaper-manufacturing business, but, unsatisfied with the business world, he moved to Philadelphia in 1823 to work as a wood engraver and pursue his art. He was largely self-taught from books and gallery visits. In the spring of 1825, he moved to New York City. That same summer he visited the Hudson Valley for the first time and made three paintings near the recently opened Catskill Mountain House. He sold them to the influential artist Colonel John Trumbull, and his career as a landscape painter was launched.

Cole made his first sketching trip to the eastern edge of the Adirondacks in 1826, visiting Glens Falls, Lake George, and Fort Ticonderoga. During 1826–27, he used these sketches to create four popular paintings illustrating scenes from James Fennimore Cooper's *Last of the Mohicans* (1826). In 1830, he executed seven paintings to illustrate John Howard Hinton's *The History and Topography of the United States*, three of which featured scenes from the Champlain Valley. He made the first of several excursions to the Schroon Lake area in 1835. One of the best-known paintings from these visits, *View of Schroon Mountain*, was completed in 1838.[1]

Cole's influential "Essay on American Scenery" was published in *American Monthly Magazine* in January 1836, resulting in requests by aspiring artists to study painting with him. Frederic Church was his student from 1844 until 1846. During the summer of 1846, Cole took his last sketching trip through the central Adirondacks, including visits to the Iron Works and Long Lake. He was accompanied on that

1. Louis Legrand Noble, *The Life and Works of Thomas Cole* (1964; reprint, Hendersonville, NY: Black Dome Press, 1997). An excellent summary of Cole's career and significance as an artist is in Kevin J. Avery, "Thomas Cole (1801–1848)," Aug. 2009, Heilbrunn Timeline of Art History, Metropolitan Museum of Art, http://www.metmuseum.org/toah/hd/cole/hd_cole.htm.

trip by Benjamin McConkey, a student from Ohio, and Louis Legrand Noble, his pastor and eventual biographer from Catskill, New York. They were guided by the noted Adirondack guide John Cheney, whom McEntee would soon meet during his own visit to the Iron Works. Two finished paintings Cole made of Long Lake were known to have existed but are now lost.[2] Thomas Cole died of pleurisy on February 11, 1848, at the age of forty-eight.

McEntee never met Cole, but because Church had studied intensively with Cole, he likely discussed his mentor's work with McEntee. McEntee was surely familiar with Cole's paintings and would necessarily have discussed "Essay on American Scenery" with Church. This letter contains brief quotations from that essay worked into McEntee's narrative.

Based on McEntee's description, the falls he and Tubby sketched must have been Buttermilk Falls, now a popular tourist stop near where the Raquette River enters the south end of Long Lake. The day after they completed their waterfall sketches, the party embarked on the road to the Iron Works. The man hired to transport their baggage was Zenas Parker, the same man who moved their baggage from Brandreth Lake to Raquette Lake and, according to the 1850 census, a near neighbor of Austin.[3]

2. Noble, *Life and Works of Thomas Cole*, 279–81.

3. Ancestry.com, 1850 United States Federal Census (online database), 2009, https://www.ancestry.com/search/collections/8054/; original data on Zenas Parker from Seventh Census of the United States, 1850, residence date: 1850, home in 1850: Long Lake, Hamilton, NY, Records of the Bureau of the Census, Record Group 29, series M432, roll 511, p. 27a, National Archives.

Part Three | High Peaks

**Long Lake to the High Peaks to the Schroon River,
Then Home to Rondout via Lowville**

August 1:	On foot on road to Bissell's Inn at Pendleton (Newcomb), then by wagon on road to Cheney's at Lower Iron Works—25 miles
August 2:	On foot on road to Upper Iron Works—10 miles
August 4:	On foot by trail to Henderson Lake—1 mile
August 2, 6, 8, and 11:	Hikes to the Indian Pass, about 4 miles one way
August 12–13:	Climb up Mount Marcy, about 11 miles one way
August 18:	By lumber wagon on road to Root's Hotel at Schroon River—30 miles

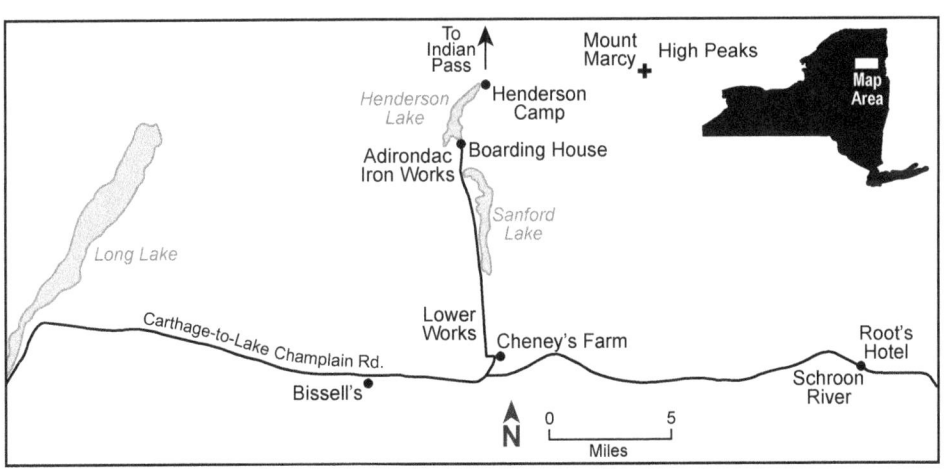

M.3. Map for part three. Joseph W. Stoll, Syracuse University Cartographic Laboratory.

The Trip to Cheney's at the Lower Iron Works

To Mr. and Mrs. James S. McEntee,
Clovertop, Rondout, New York
Friday, August 1, 1851

Dear Father, dear Mother,

You will be pleased to know that we arrived safely at the Iron Works this afternoon. We are staying at the house of the mighty hunter John Cheney. His wife, Lucinda, is as friendly and talkative as her husband and a very good cook.

    We left Long Lake this morning directly after breakfast. Parker, Austin's nearest neighbor, came last night with his horse and cart to pick up our baggage, so we walked briskly along the road carrying only our guns. As we left, I asked Austin whether he knew of somewhere I could acquire new boots. Despite the repairs effected by Robinson only a short time ago, mine remained in very poor condition. Austin told me there might be a man in Lumberville who would have some boots to sell. Expecting to come upon a small village somewhere along the way, we passed right by the place he called "Lumberville" without notice since it consisted of only a large house and barn in a new clearing.

    By walking steadily, we arrived at Bissell's Inn about 1 o'clock. The village of Pendleton, called Newcomb by some, was settled a long time ago as there are extensive clearings stretching for three to four miles along the road, some with good frame houses and prosperous-looking farms. Although a fair number of families live here now, many of the old clearings are growing up again with a dense growth of wild cherry.

Bissell's is the first proper inn that we have encountered since we left Lowville more than seven weeks ago. "Everything looked thrifty here, the house appearing very much like those of our Ulster farmers." After we ordered our dinner, Professor Benedict came in and his party dined with us. They were bound for Racket Lake, where they planned to stay a few weeks. They had come up from Root's in the Schroon Valley.

Since the wagon that brought the Benedicts was set to return empty and would pass directly by the Lower Iron Works, where we were bound, we sent Parker on his way home and transferred our baggage. We had gone on about a mile when Josiah discovered he had left his hat behind at Bissell's and had to run back to get it.

As we rode slowly along, I could not help but notice that we were entering a more settled territory. Before long we were driving by the upper reaches of the Hudson River, here just a meandering shallow stream. There are large piles of logs along the riverbank waiting for the spring freshet that will float them to market. In between Pendleton and the Iron Works the once unbroken forest is thin and patchy since most of the pine has been cut out.

After we were settled at Cheney's and had a good supper, I asked Cheney if he knew of a place in the village where I might buy boots. He said a man named Shaw keeps a supply of boots, clothes and such at his house to sell. My feet were awfully painful after the long walk from Austin's. In hope of finally finding a remedy, I decided to immediately pay Mr. Shaw a visit.

The village of the Lower Iron Works is not far from Cheney's. I expected to find a substantial settlement, but there is only an unoccupied frame hotel, a dozen log houses, a dam, a sawmill, a limekiln and a number of charcoal pits. Shaw was at home and at long last I was able to obtain a heavy pair of new boots. They are slightly too large for my feet, a condition I have sought to remedy somewhat by a new pair of thick stockings.

Thanks to my new boots the walk back to Cheney's was a pleasant one. The boots are stout, well made and appear suited for hard use. Should I ever undertake another wilderness sketching trip, I will forgo all fashion in footwear and instead acquire boots like these, rough workmen's boots that can be used hard and that will dependably protect my feet.

Tomorrow we will move on to the Upper Iron Works, also called Adirondac, where we will set up camp at a lake on the edge of town to prepare for our visits to the Indian Pass and the high mountains.

Due to unexpected expenses, my supply of money is now very low. Please send a further modest remittance to the post office here if at all possible.

Your obedient son,
Jervis

Notes for Letter 23

The travelers departed Long Lake on foot on August 1. The distance from Austin's farm at Long Lake to the village of Pendleton was about seventeen miles on the Carthage–to–Lake Champlain Road. Today's NY Route 28N follows essentially the same course. They intended to reach Bissell's Inn in the settlement of Pendleton in time for dinner. Since they were unencumbered, they would have been reasonably able to walk there in about four to five hours.

In 1808, Nathaniel Pendleton bought five thousand acres near Rich Lake along the upper Hudson River. The settlement that grew up adjacent to his farm was originally named for him. When the town was incorporated in 1828, the inhabitants intended to name it "Pendleton"; however, a town named "Pendleton" had already been chartered in Niagara County the previous year. Accordingly, the town was named "Newcomb" for the family with the largest land holdings in the area. The settlement was still commonly referred to as "Pendleton" until 1863, when the Newcomb Post Office was established.

McEntee's party took their dinner at Bissell's, known to locals as "Aunt Polly's Inn," one of the central Adirondack's earliest hostelries. The inn was founded sometime after 1827, when Daniel Bissell married Polly Butler, daughter of William Butler, a prominent early settler.[1]

While at Bissell's, McEntee noted they had dinner with Professor Benedict and his traveling companions, who had just arrived. This was Farrand N. Benedict, professor of mathematics at the University of Vermont. Benedict had been exploring the central Adirondacks since 1835. In 1837, he was the first to accurately calculate the height of Mount Marcy. Benedict was an early proponent of a railroad through the central Adirondacks, but his plans repeatedly met with failure. Beginning in the late 1840s, he and his partners began to acquire large

---

1. Much of this information comes from informal discussions with Don Seauvageau, president of the Newcomb Historical Museum Board of Trustees, McEntee's 1851 journal, and genealogical information gleaned from Ancestry.com. A detailed history of the founding of Pendleton is set forth in Raymond D. Masters, *A Social History of the Huntington Wildlife Forest* (Utica, NY: North Country, 1993), 13–22.

forest tracts for logging. To reach lucrative markets in the Hudson Valley, Benedict wanted to build a dam at the foot of Long Lake to raise the water level about twenty feet, then construct a canal from the north end of Long Lake to Round Pond in the upper Hudson River watershed. A short section of the projected canal was constructed before the entire project was abandoned.[2]

McEntee does not seem to have known any of this. He apparently also did not know that Professor Benedict was the owner of 152,000 acres of the land surrounding Raquette Lake. When McEntee met the Benedict party at Bissell's in 1851, Professor Benedict was on his way to Raquette Lake to supervise a group of his students who intended to survey his property. That summer, Benedict was accompanied by his wife, Elizabeth Ogden, and his younger brothers, William, Joel, and Abner.[3]

It may seem surprising that McEntee saw stacks of felled trees along the banks of the upper Hudson River in early August as they approached the Lower Iron Works. Trees were usually cut in winter and moved to where they would be floated to market the following spring. By August, any trees cut the prior winter would have already disappeared downstream, but McEntee recorded that he saw quite a bit of cut timber between the road and the river.[4] The fact that the Iron Works required large amounts of charcoal year-round for operation of the furnaces may account for the piles of timber McEntee observed. Later the same day McEntee would see charcoal pits at the Lower Iron Works, where trees were converted into charcoal.

2. The remains of this canal are described in Benson J. Lossing, *The Hudson from the Wilderness to the Sea* (1866; reprint, Somersworth, NH: New Hampshire Publishing, 1972), 14–16; see also Mike Prescott, "Ferrand Benedict's Abandoned Newcomb–Long Lake Canal," *Adirondack Almanack*, June 11, 2016, https://www.adirondack almanack.com/2016/06/short-biography-farrad-benedict-conclusion.html.

3. See Barbara McMartin, *To the Lake of the Skies: The Benedicts in the Adirondacks* (Chicago: Lakeview Press, 1996), 15–36.

4. McEntee, "Journal of the 1851 Adirondack Sketching Trip," typed transcript, 77.

Meeting the Famous Guide John Cheney

To Miss Augusta McEntee, Clovertop, Rondout, New York
Wednesday, August 2, 1851

Dear Gussie,

Because your letters to me have evinced so much enthusiasm for hearing about the woodsmen we are meeting, I will tell you a little of John Cheney, perhaps the most famous Adirondack woodsman now alive. He lives with his wife, Lucinda, on a new farm at a place called the Lower Iron Works, or Tahawus, fast by the road we have followed much of the way on our adventure. He was not home when we first arrived but came in presently, having been to his springhouse for water. I was relieved to find that he had room to keep us for the night since we were tired and had already unloaded our baggage from the wagon that brought us.

I have strongly desired to meet Cheney ever since I read about his exploits in Headley's book, where he is hailed as a "mighty hunter." Expecting a grizzled old woodsman, I was surprised that he is small and light of body, with a pleasing countenance and friendly manner. He helped us move our baggage inside, inquired of our journey, etc., all the time making us feel very welcome. I noticed that he was a little lame, which he explained was on account of a fall from a tree that he had last winter.

I asked him straightaway whether there was anywhere I could buy new boots as mine had become almost useless. He assured me that a man named Shaw, the overseer of the Lower Works, would have some. After partaking of an excellent supper, Cheney walked down with us to Shaw's store, next to the village wharf about a mile distant, because he needed to bring his cows home from a meadow near there. Shaw had a supply of boots to sell, so at last I acquired a sturdy pair, which will surely make the remainder of the trip more tolerable.

As we walked back to his farm driving the cows ahead of us, Cheney told us with great feeling the story of the accidental shooting death of Mr. David Henderson, one of the mine owners, five years ago. It appears that while hunting Henderson dropped his pistol, and as it was already cocked to fire, it discharged, hitting him at point-blank range. Cheney was a member of the party and was the one who arranged for the body to be brought out of the woods.

After we arrived back at Cheney's farm, I settled into a chair by the front window, only to find a copy of Headley's book on a little side table there. As I sat reading by the light of the sunset, a wagon arrived with two Harvard students seeking lodging. Cheney said he could make room for them and proceeded to help his wife get their supper.

After the students had supper, "Cheney and Puffer who were old friends sat in the kitchen and each listened to the other's hunting stories which attracted our Harvard boys into the circle who listened with great satisfaction." Cheney told of how he had been guiding in these mountains for more than twenty years. He told of all the game he had killed using his pistol rather than a rifle and proudly claimed he never killed an animal but that it was needed for food. He told of a time when hunting a deer from a boat how he accidentally shot himself in the leg, quickly bound up the wound, continued hunting and was still able to walk home.

After many more of such stories, "Cheney, knowing the wakefulness of novices in wood life, disposing us for bed marched us to our rooms." Puffer, Josiah and the Harvard boys slept in a room upstairs. Joe and I occupied a small room downstairs. For a time, we listened to excited conversations from above until at long last we fell asleep.

This morning we arranged with Shaw for our baggage to be transported to the Upper Iron Works by boat. We therefore set out up the road empty-handed. It was a fine, clear day. We passed the ten-mile walk very pleasantly, talking and joking, aided by partaking of handfuls of ripe raspberries that grow thickly all along the way.

We plan to remain in these parts for the next two weeks. Please write back when you can. It is a great comfort to hear news from home.

Affectionately, your brother,

Jervis

Notes for Letter 24

This letter is devoted primarily to McEntee's description of John and Lucinda Cheney. McEntee consistently misspelled Cheney's name as "Cheeney" in his journal. To avoid any confusion, I have used the correct spelling, without the extra *e*, in the letters. McEntee apparently first learned about Cheney from reading Joel Headley's book, where he was first labeled a "mighty hunter." John Cheney (1800–1877), one of the earliest guides of the High Peaks region, was highly praised in many accounts.[1]

Daniel and Polly Bissell's eldest daughter, Lucinda, had by 1851 married John Cheney and was living with him at the Lower Iron Works. When the artists visited in 1851, the Cheneys were living in a new frame house on a one-hundred-acre farm located about a mile east of Lower Works. Travelers celebrated Lucinda Bissell Cheney as a great cook and nonstop conversationalist. The Cheneys later became the proprietors of the boardinghouse at the Lower Works and called it the "Tahawus House." They ran it as a hotel until it burned to the ground in 1874.[2]

At the Lower Works, McEntee was finally able to obtain new boots from Thomas Shaw. At the time of the 1850 census, Shaw was the proprietor of the boardinghouse at the Lower Works. Later, in October 1850, Andrew Porteous resigned as superintendent of the Lower Iron Works, the workers were laid off, and the boardinghouse closed. When McEntee visited in August 1851, Shaw was one of the few remaining inhabitants of the Lower Works, where he operated a store and served as caretaker for the company property.[3]

1. Headley, *The Adirondack*, 75–84. For other accounts, see, for example, Hoffman, *Wild Scenes from the Forest and Prairie*, 1:35–42, and Seneca Ray Stoddard, *The Adirondacks, Illustrated* (Albany, NY: Weed, Parsons, 1874), 114–17.

2. An excellent account of Cheney's work as a guide is given in George Marshall, "Adirondack Guides of the High Peaks," in *The Adirondack High Peaks and the Forty-Sixers*, ed. Grace Hudowalski (Albany, NY: Peters Print, 1970), 105–31. The hunting stories Cheney told are here adapted from Arthur H. Masten, *The Story of Adirondac* (Syracuse, NY: Syracuse Univ. Press, 1968), 157–67.

3. Masten, *The Story of Adirondac*, 134.

Cheney's first-person account of the accidental shooting death of David Henderson can be found in Arthur H. Masten's *The Story of Adirondac* (1968).[4] Cheney was present at the scene and appears to bear some responsibility for the accident because he was the one who handed Henderson the loaded and cocked pistol. Henderson had become the manager of the Iron Works in 1838 and held that position until his death in September 1845.

4. Masten, *The Story of Adirondac*, 99–105. An almost identical account appeared in Alfred L. Donaldson, *A History of the Adirondacks* (1921; unabridged reprint, Fleischmanns, NY: Purple Mountain Press, 1996), 1:143–46.

Impressions of the Adirondac Iron Works

To Miss Julia McEntee, c/o Mr. Charles McEntee,
Rondout, New York
Sunday, August 3, 1851

Dear Cousin Julia,

I'm writing to you from the sitting room of the workman's boardinghouse at a place known as Adirondac village, or the Upper Iron
Works. We arrived here yesterday and intended to depart this morning but our baggage was not delivered as promised so Puffer and I
had to row down the lake today to retrieve it. That tiresome task
occupied us all day. We will set up our camp on a lake a mile outside
the village tomorrow.

   You probably recall that one of my primary artistic goals for this
trip was to observe and sketch the Great Indian Pass as shown so
dramatically in Ingham's famous painting. We arrived at this village yesterday in the early afternoon and immediately departed up
the trail to the Indian Pass. As we first approached the Pass, I could
see that it was worth all the effort we had expended. We climbed
through the Pass until I stood at the very spot where Ingham had
sketched. It was the most magnificent picture I ever saw. We plan to
return for as many days as it takes for us to complete studies for our
future paintings.

   Finding an iron works here in the wilderness is interesting in
itself. A great deposit of iron ore was discovered here many years
ago but owing to the remoteness of the place it took a long time to
construct the means to extract it. The original owners first needed
to clear a road through unbroken forest. When that task was complete, they built a dam to extend an existing lake so that supplies

ADIRONDAC IRON WORKS

3.1. Jervis McEntee, *The Iron Works*, wood engraving by Loomis-Annin from sketch by Jervis McEntee. In Jervis McEntee, "The Lakes of the Wilderness," *Great Republic Monthly*, Apr. 1, 1859, 348. Courtesy of the American Antiquarian Society, Worcester, MA.

and finished iron could be transported by water from the mine ten miles to the road. That task completed, an iron works and a village were built.

I have been told by the current superintendent of the works that for a number of years the place flourished. By 1843 they were producing up to fourteen tons of iron a day. At that time the Upper Works village had sixteen buildings, a school and a large boardinghouse for workers that could number in the hundreds. A second village had grown up at the lower end of the lake where there was a second furnace that could make steel.

When we stopped at the Lower Iron Works, also known as Tahawus, this past Friday it was mostly abandoned. The works there

are shut down and the boardinghouse stands empty. We were told
by the overseer that the decline started with the untimely accidental
death of the managing partner of the business, Mr. David Henderson. I have written more about what I learned about this sad event in
a letter I sent to Gussie yesterday.

There can be no doubt that the possibility of making a profit
from extracting the good-quality iron here is what leads the company
to persevere in the effort. A new iron furnace is under construction
near here and there is talk of a new road or even a railroad to make
transport of the heavy iron more feasible. How this put me in mind
of the great effort father expended in the Pennsylvania coal fields
when I was a little boy. Perhaps if a talented and vigorous engineer
can be found, success will come at last to this place.

The Adirondac village is located in quite a beautiful place and
because the buildings are constructed with mountains all around it
has an alpine look. I took a quick sketch of it, which I have pasted to
this letter in order for you to form a better idea of it.

There is a post office in the store here. I have already received
some newspapers, including a recent number of the Rondout Courier
with one of my letters in it. I have not yet received any letters from
home here, so one from you would be most welcome.

Affectionately, your cousin,

Jervis

Notes for Letter 25

McEntee obtained much of his information about the Adirondac Iron Works in conversation with Alexander Ralph, the agent of the company at the Upper Works and an amateur artist.[1]

Development of the Iron Works began in the early 1830s but was frustrated by numerous logistical problems. It was not until after the state geologist Ebenezer Emmons visited the area in 1837 and reported what he saw as the unrivaled possibilities of the McIntyre ore beds that investors gained the confidence to commit to a major effort to achieve success.

David Henderson became the consistent driving force behind building up the Iron Works. He was appointed the general manager of the works in 1838. After he died in September 1845, progress slowed and then stopped when economic conditions worsened. In the 1850 census, the Lower Iron Works, also known as Tahawus, had twelve households with eighty residents, including seventeen living in the boardinghouse run by Thomas Shaw.[2] Less than a year later when McEntee visited, the Lower Works had ceased operations, and the boardinghouse was closed. Operations continued at the Upper Iron Works, but the owners were more interested in trying to sell the Iron Works than in making iron. A new furnace was completed at the Upper Works in 1854, but profitability did not improve. The Iron

1. The colorful first-person account written by David Henderson of how Lewis Elijah Benedict led the founders of the Adirondac Iron Works to the ore bed in 1826 is included in Masten, *The Story of Adirondac*, 17–26. A more accessible reproduction of Henderson's letter can be found in *The Adirondack Reader*, ed. Jamieson with Burdick, 58–61.

2. Information on Thomas Shaw at the Lower Works comes from Ancestry.com, 1850 United States Federal Census (online database), 2009, https://www.ancestry.com /search/collections/8054/; original data from Seventh Census of the United States, 1650, Residence Date: 1850, home in 1850: Newcomb, Essex, NY, Records of the Bureau of the Census, Record Group 29, series M432, roll 504, p. 299a, National Archives.

Works stopped production entirely in 1858, and both villages were mostly abandoned.[3]

Today the site of the Upper Works serves as an important trail-head providing access to the southern High Peaks Wilderness Area. In 2021, the Open Space Institute placed a series of illustrated plaques where the village of Adirondac once stood, presenting the history of the area.[4]

As McEntee suggests in this letter, transporting heavy iron ingots to market proved to be difficult and expensive. The only transportation was by horse-drawn wagon or sledge to Lake Champlain on a road in chronically poor repair. The heavy iron was usually moved in the winter, when the road was frozen over and comparably smooth. Although not mentioned in the journal, this problem, I believe, would have reminded McEntee of his father's work in 1830 at the coal mines in Carbondale, Pennsylvania.

3. An extensive history of the Iron Works based on original sources can be found in Masten, *The Story of Adirondac*. Also see H. Perry Smith, *History of Essex County* (Syracuse, NY: D. Mason, 1885), 641–51.

4. The Open Space Institute website describes the plaque project at https://www.openspaceinstitute.org/news/open-space-institute-announces-completion-of-adirondac-upper-works-project-to-improve-public-access-in-the-adirondacks.

John Cheney's Artist Story

To Miss Mary McEntee, Clovertop, Rondout, New York
Sunday, August 3, 1851

Dearest sister Mary,

I hope I can correctly assume that you have already had the opportunity to read my recent letters to our parents, our cousin Julia and Gussie that describe my current whereabouts. Yesterday we walked about ten miles from Cheney's house at the Lower Iron Works to the Upper Iron Works, called Adirondac by local folks. We left our baggage in a storeroom near the dock at the Lower Works and made arrangements for it to be transported here the next morning by the boat that brings the mail and supplies.

We spent a wakeful night in rooms we rented in Wright's boardinghouse, where many of the men who work here reside, their home farms being some good distance away. At 7 o'clock the next morning I woke and went to look for the boatman to inquire of our baggage. I found him in the sitting room reading a newspaper. Seeing me, he apologized that he could not bring our things because the boat was already too heavily laden. He seemed sincere in his promise to go back for our baggage immediately after breakfast if he could get use of the boat.

Breakfast was not served until 10 a.m. Afterwards I quickly hunted down the boatman again, who said the clerk would not let him take the boat out because it was Sunday. "I began to grow impatient at the delay and vexed at the niggardly spirit of the clerk who would not accommodate us in this dilemma."

I consulted together with my companions and we all agreed that we did not want to wait until tomorrow evening for our baggage to come. At the village dock a man rented me an old square-toed scow and Puffer and I set out rowing the ten miles down the lake to retrieve our supplies. By taking turns rowing, we were able to reach our destination by 1 o'clock. We loaded our baggage and started back without stopping to have dinner.

The load was heavy and the wind was against us so it was fully 5 o'clock by the time we arrived back. Joe met us at the dock, where he had been waiting for us since 2 o'clock. Josiah appeared just as we started to unload the baggage, having been to church in the school-house with a preacher from Jersey City. Together we carried our baggage up to the boardinghouse. The boarders looked on with some amusement but they later "were unanimous in awarding us the palm for being good carriers."

While at the Lower Works I encountered Cheney, who told me of an artist who had visited here recently and bragged of his skill in camping out. This fellow claimed that the Indian Pass had never been painted properly, but he would show them how it looked on canvas. When he left Wright's boardinghouse the next day, he carried only a large knife and a frying pan. He stayed one night in the woods, then got discouraged and departed.

"He came back again however in a week or two and got Wright to go with him to the Pass and build a shanty for him where he was going to stay alone until he finished painting the Pass." After building the camp Wright returned to the village, fishing in the stream along the way, "but behold, the artist had arrived at the house ahead of him. Wright asked him several times to let him see some of his pictures but the only thing that he produced was what he called a sketch of Mt. Colden drawn on the bottom of his frying pan with the point of his knife!"

Cheney claimed he could not remember this fellow's name. As the artist left, he told Cheney that he "had heard we were coming and that he meant to get sketches of all the good scenery ahead of us. We came upon his camp in the Pass where I don't blame him for fearing to spend the night alone."

We will leave the boardinghouse tomorrow morning to set up our tent camp at a pretty lake about a mile outside the village. From there we will take our sketching boxes to the Indian Pass, where we will do our best to capture its sublime beauty. If the weather is agreeable, we will later climb Mount Tahawus before beginning our homeward journey.

I look forward to seeing you soon.

Your brother,

Jervis

Notes for Letter 26

This letter is addressed to Mary McEntee, Jervis's next younger sibling, who in a few years would marry Calvert Vaux (see letter 21 and its notes). John Cheney's story of an unnamed artist and his frying pan at the heart of this letter is without question the most peculiar entry in McEntee's trip journal. Although the story is utterly unbelievable, in telling it McEntee used the same matter-of-fact style as in all his other journal entries.

Cheney certainly had more experience with visiting artists than any other guide of the time. He was one of the guides for Ebenezer Emmons's expedition in 1837, when Charles Cromwell Ingham created his famous work *The Great Adirondack Pass, Painted on the Spot.* Cheney also guided Thomas Cole on his sketching trip in 1846 that included a trip to the Indian Pass. Meeting McEntee and Tubby probably provided the stimulus for Cheney to invent a fanciful story that illustrated his opinion of artists who ventured into the wilderness.

The story clearly shows that Cheney felt some artists he had guided did not appreciate the difficulties involved in making a sketching trip to the High Peaks wilderness. It was reported, for example, that while being guided by Cheney, Ingham fainted owing to the exertion required to hike to the Indian Pass.[1] It's also possible that Cheney had guided for artists who had brashly claimed or implied that they had outdoor skills that they plainly lacked. Cheney may also have felt that some artists, like the mystery artist in the story, were unjustified in their inflated opinion of their artistic abilities.[2]

It is thus quite possible that the story was wholly fanciful, invented by Cheney just to amuse McEntee. According to all the early writers who met Cheney, he was not opposed to stretching the truth for the

1. Sandra Hildreth, "Finding 'The Great Adirondack Pass,'" *Adirondack Almanack*, Apr. 5, 2012, https://www.adirondackalmanack.com/2012/04/sandy-hildreth -finding-the-great-adirondack-pass.html.

2. Masten, *The Story of Adirondac*, 157–67; see also Marshall, "Adirondack Guides," 110–15, and Hoffman, *Wild Scenes from the Forest and Prairie*, 35–47.

sake of a good story. Many of Cheney's stories were so interesting or charming that they were carefully recorded by visitors such as Charles Fenno Hoffman, Joel T. Headley, and S. R. Stoddard. The story of the mystery artist, however, appears only in McEntee's journal. If Cheney told it to anyone else, they did not write it down.[3]

In McEntee's trip journal, Cheney's story is set out without commentary about its believability. It's possible, of course, that McEntee just naively believed the story, disregarding its improbability. There are clues, however, that McEntee himself invented all or parts of the story. He easily could have added the story to his trip journal at the time he transcribed it.

One part of the story possibly invented by McEntee is the claim that the unnamed artist somehow knew McEntee and Tubby were coming to paint the Indian Pass and so wanted to get there first. This is highly unlikely since only McEntee's family and close acquaintances knew of his trip and its artistic objectives. If the artist in the story knew McEntee's plans, he would have been someone known to McEntee. The fact that the name of the mystery artist is omitted is an indication that McEntee added this part of the story.

Suggesting that a competing artist was rushing to paint the scene serves to show how important McEntee thought his painting of the Indian Pass might be when it was unveiled to his fellow artists on his return to New York City. This point is further highlighted by having the mystery artist allegedly claim the Indian Pass had never been properly painted. This may have been McEntee's actual opinion of the earlier paintings of the pass after his visits to the site.

McEntee may have tried to make the story seem more plausible by giving a role to Wright, the boardinghouse proprietor he had met his first day at the Upper Iron Works. McEntee necessarily had to have

---

3. Accounts of visits with Cheney invariably included examples of his storytelling. A good selection of Cheney's stories can be found in Hoffman, *Wild Scenes from the Forest and Prairie*, 35–47; Headley, *The Adirondack*, 75–84; Lossing, *The Hudson from the Wilderness to the Sea*, 46–48; and Stoddard, *The Adirondacks, Illustrated*, 117–22.

added the detail that he saw the shanty that Wright allegedly built for the unnamed artist at the Indian Pass. It's possible that McEntee did see a shanty there, but if he did, he didn't mention it in any of his other descriptions of their four visits to sketch the pass.

I believe that McEntee included this story in his trip journal because he planned to use it in some later writing that would show his critics that his sketching trip, unlike that of the mystery artist, had certainly not been a fool's errand. His sketches and paintings would be proof of that. The fact that the story mocks an artist who falsely claimed to possess the requisite outdoor skills could be contrasted with the fact that by this point in the trip McEntee and Tubby had worked hard to acquire all those necessary skills. Indeed, at several points in the journal McEntee notes that although some of his acquaintances had doubted that he would be able to complete the trip, the outdoorsmen they met remarked on how well he and Joe were managing.

McEntee ultimately did write, illustrate, and publish "The Lakes of the Wilderness" (1859), a somewhat fictionalized account of the trip. He did not include the artist-with-a-frying-pan story in that article, possibly because when he did exhibit his finished painting of the Indian Pass, it did not attract the acclaim that he felt it deserved.

Sketching at the Indian Pass

To Mr. Frederic E. Church, the American
Art-Union Bldg., New York, New York
Sunday, August 10, 1851

Dear Mr. Church,

We had our first glimpse of the fabled Indian Pass a week ago last
Sunday. Oh, how I had dreamed of that moment! A difficult trail
leads from the village of Adirondac along a small stream to the Pass.
"After walking a long time, we began to catch occasional glimpses
of the wonder through the trees, holding its jagged masses of rocks
above us in the open sky and forming an outline upon the blue that
I trembled to look upon. Yet we were a long distance off and the
nearer we approached the more tremendous it appeared. At the foot
of where the precipice first commences, we stopped at a spring and
drank. From here we got the best view of it looking east although it
was somewhat obstructed by the intervening foliage. Up it sprang
from our feet, a perpendicular wall of broken rock trembling above
us two thousand feet in the air, its hard and rugged outline down-
ward again away beyond us. All around us lay huge rocks that had
thundered down from the steep in the forgotten ages and now lichen-
ous and gray rested in the wild gorge. Such a scene of grandeur, of
sublimity and wildness I had not anticipated and it far surpassed my
wildest and most fanciful imaginings."

That first trip was but a preliminary foray undertaken in the
afternoon and not allowing any time for sketching. I must say it was a
thrill to stand in the exact spot where Ingham stood back in '37 as he
worked on the sketch for his famous painting. I thought back to our
winter days together and recollected the story you heard from the

venerable Cole of his impressions of this same scene. As we trudged back to the village, a pleasurable feeling of finally reaching a long-sought goal washed over me.

We intended to return with our sketching tools as soon as we were able but first we had to attend to setting up camp. This task took longer than expected. On the first day we were free from other duties it rained all day, requiring us to sit in camp in lazy anxiety.

Wednesday dawned gray, but by the time we finished our breakfast, the sky had cleared. Joe and I with Puffer's help carried our sketching supplies the four miles back to the Indian Pass. Puffer brought along an axe so as to cut down trees to improve the view. We selected a good scene after clambering over the rocks to look over a few candidates. Puffer presently returned to camp while Joe and I set to work on our sketches at last.

We sketched until the sun began to slip behind the mountains that overshadow the Pass. "There was the same soft light upon the hills that enveloped them the first time I saw them. 'Sandanona' and 'Panther' Mountain, on which the soft blue shadows slept, bounded the view and between them and the precipice the lesser hills swelled out their wooded sides which towards evening presented the richest color I had ever seen. The sun was going down behind them, leaving all but the edges and summits in shade, that deep dreamy shade that cannot be painted or described but must be seen to be felt. When the light stole along the tops it made them almost of a golden hue and darting in among the dark masses of evergreens on the ridge of the mountain nearest the precipice gave an almost enchanting effect to the view. It is one of those wild scenes so full of majesty and sublimity which the Creator has formed for us to look upon that we may better comprehend his boundless power, and yet they who look upon it must endure no little toil for the privilege, for its gateway is of the rugged rock and the tangled forest and the feet [that] pass through it are few as the hardily discernible path will attest."

Rain on Thursday kept us in camp again, but Friday found us back at the Pass hard at work. It rained again on Saturday. Joe was not feeling well today, so I made a sketch of the village similar in composition to the one by Cole you showed me. If the weather is tolerable tomorrow, we will return to the Pass one final time to finish our sketches.

How I wish you were here to share in this endeavor. I will come to New York as soon as I'm able to show you the results of my artistic labors.

Sincerely, your friend,
Jervis

Notes for Letter 27

McEntee's journal makes clear that making sketches of the Indian Pass was one of the main artistic objectives of the trip. He and Tubby visited the pass on four separate days even though the trail was a difficult one. McEntee recorded his impressions of the pass at length in his journal, portions of which are included in this letter.

Entries in McEntee's journal clearly indicate he was familiar with the painting of the Indian Pass made by Charles Cromwell Ingham. In August 1837, Ingham was part of the group accompanying the state geologist Ebenezer Emmons to make illustrations for the geologic portion of the state's Natural History Survey. The John H. Bufford lithograph based on Ingham's painting of the pass was published in Emmons's widely read *New York State Natural History Survey Report* of 1838.[1] Ingham's dramatic painting of the scene, titled *The Great Adirondack Pass, Painted on the Spot*, was exhibited at the National Academy of Design in 1839. It is now in the collection of The Adirondack Experience, The Museum on Blue Mountain Lake.

Ingham intended his painting to be accepted as a faithful rendering of the Indian Pass even though the painting was named *The Great Adirondack Pass*. McEntee certainly thought it faithfully described the scene as he gazed at the pass from approximately the same spot where Ingham had made his sketches fourteen years earlier. Interestingly, Ingham's painting exaggerates parts of the landscape to increase its dramatic effect.[2]

The sketches McEntee and Tubby made at the pass and their subsequent paintings of the scene are not known presently to exist. However, an undated oil painting by McEntee titled *Mountain Mist in the Morning* bears a resemblance to Thomas Cole's sketches and Ingham's painting of the pass. This painting could possibly be one of McEntee's

---

1. Ebenezer Emmons, *New York State Natural History Survey Report* (Albany: State of New York, 1838).

2. See Hildreth, "Finding 'The Great Adirondack Pass.'"

painted sketches of the Indian Pass, but there is no direct evidence to support this speculation.

McEntee's journal does not indicate whether he knew that Thomas Cole visited the Indian Pass on a sketching trip in 1846, but it seems likely that Church knew of that trip and of Cole's sketches. Cole's realistic pencil sketches of the Indian Pass are now in the collection of the Detroit Institute of Arts. There is no direct evidence that Church showed any of Cole's sketches to McEntee. A side-by-side comparison of McEntee's and Cole's sketches of the village of Adirondac do show remarkable similarities.

Climbing Tahawus (Mount Marcy)

To Nathaniel B. Sylvester, Esq., N. State St., Lowville, New York
Thursday, August 14, 1851

Dear friend Sylvester,

We are nearing the end of our sketching trip at long last. I trust I will
see you again in person in a week or so when I return to Lowville
with Puffer to retrieve those items we left behind at the outset of
our trip. At present I am resting my knee in our camp at Henderson
Lake a mile outside of the village of Adirondac. As you know, I was
determined to see the view from the top of Mount Tahawus before
departing for home. We achieved that goal yesterday; however, the
climb proved to be quite arduous and along the way I had the misfortune of injuring my knee.

  We began our ascent of the mountain early this past Tuesday
morning. We first carried some of our baggage down to the village
and left it at the boardinghouse since we did not anticipate needing it
again before departing for home, which we planned to do as soon as
possible on returning from Tahawus.

  In the village we chanced to meet Mr. Clark, a local man who has
climbed Tahawus a number of times. He gave us helpful directions
and even accompanied us for the first half mile to where the trail
begins. The trail is modestly well used for the six miles to Calamity
Pond, where Mr. Henderson was killed. We stopped to rest at the
dam and to fish for trout for dinner. While crossing the stream there,
I slipped on a stone and fell, twisting my knee. I rested for an hour or
so at the shanty nearby. My injury was painful but did not completely
hobble me. For a time I considered turning back, but having already
come so far I decided to go on.

The beaten trail thinned and then ended after we made our way to the other side of the pond. We pressed on through thick brush and over rocks for the next mile until we came to a stream picturesquely called the Opalescent River. We followed up this stream a short distance to reach Lake Colden, one of the most romantic sheets of water I have ever seen, with mountains rising steeply from both its sides.

We continued to ascend along the Opalescent for four to five miles, where it turned northeast. A mile further on we reached a well-constructed open camp near where the forest gives way to bare rock. Puffer cooked the trout he caught earlier for our supper. As soon as it was fully dark, we wrapped ourselves in our blankets and fell asleep three thousand feet above sea level.

We had our breakfast at first light. Leaving our belongings behind at the shanty we were soon climbing over bare rock towards the peak. "Near the top we drank from a good spring, after leaving which we walked on the smooth, slanting rock and stood upon the summit of Tahawus, the spot to which my heart had often turned in its longings and which I had one day hoped to reach. The wind blew a gale which completely chilled us through, and the fierce clouds came trooping swiftly by us, now hiding the world below and now revealing the vast extent of country that lay stretched out at our feet. Away to the south were mountains rosy with the morning light and nearer ones lay reposing in its gray shadow. Gleaming lakes and dim valleys stretched far away and the sad and solemn gloom of the unbroken forest sent not a sound from its vast abodes below to that still summit where we stood. I shall never forget that desolate mountain top with its frowning rocks and deep impressive stillness of the summit. We had not looked long when the mist shut everything from our sight."

Puffer built us a fire and we waited on the summit for five hours but the skies did not clear. We were all dreadfully cold so at last decided to descend. We were back at the shanty in time for a hasty dinner of coffee and bread. Even though we stopped to make a quick sketch of Lake Colden, we arrived safely back at the village by 6 o'clock.

summer here
nd a number
l the life ex-
iany fearless
the ascent of

embarked in
low,
dis-
n.
wild
shall
rage
The
ough
ject
ling
ntly
upon
iany
e is
and
ider-
upon
eam
ght-
ying
plea-
the
abre
hear
r in
m to

y or
the
king

glimpse of civilization;
moreover, it was pleas-
ant, as Asa said, to
sleep in a civilized bed,
and to have a woman
pour the tea at meals.
We shot our last deer

Loomis-Annin.

MOUNT TAHAWUS.

3.2. Jervis McEntee, *Mount Tahawus*, wood engraving by Loomis-Annin from sketch by Jervis McEntee. In McEntee, "The Lakes of the Wilderness," 347. Courtesy of the American Antiquarian Society, Worcester, MA.

LAKE COLDEN

3.3. Jervis McEntee, *Lake Colden*, wood engraving by Loomis-Annin from sketch by Jervis McEntee. In McEntee, "The Lakes of the Wilderness," 347. Courtesy of the American Antiquarian Society, Worcester, MA.

I am determined to rest here in camp until my knee is better, then with regret depart the wilderness. I look forward to seeing you again soon.

Your friend,
Jervis

Notes for Letter 28

The person who provided Puffer with important details about the best trail to the summit of Mount Marcy was Robert Clarke, an official of the Adirondac Iron Works and a devoted recreational climber who is credited with the first ascent of Mount Colden, which he made with his friend Alexander Ralph, another manager whom McEntee met and admired. The route Clarke recommended was already well known by 1851 and still exists in large part today as the Calamity Brook Trail. The McEntee party did not stick to the course of the present-day trail but bypassed Lake Tear of the Clouds by continuing along the Opalescent River to an existing open camp. McEntee observed the camp was three thousand feet above sea level, but based on later, more accurate measurements it was probably higher than four thousand feet.[1]

The artists had expended great effort to reach the summit of Mount Marcy, McEntee limping during the climb, only to be frustrated by clouds rolling in and obscuring the view. They waited for hours, but the clouds never parted. Based on his brief impressions, McEntee must have decided that the scene from the summit was so sublime that he would go again and so made the arduous climb on two subsequent Adirondack sketching trips in 1863 and 1866. Shortly after his trip in 1863, he completed a painting of the view from Mount Marcy that was included in the National Academy of Design exhibition of the same year, but it has not survived. A description of that painting is included in the conclusion of this book.

1. See Weber, *Mount Marcy*, 60–61.

Departure of the Tubby Brothers

To Miss Anna Gertrude Sawyer, c/o Dr. Thomas Jefferson Sawyer,
principal, the Clinton Liberal Institute, Clinton, New York
Saturday, August 16, 1851

Dear Gertrude,

Today I started making preparations to begin my homeward journey so this will be my last letter to you from the wild northern forest. We have been camped along Henderson Lake near the Adirondac Iron Works for the past two weeks. The entire area is surrounded by the high Adirondack mountains, making for some of the most sublime scenery possible.

Happily, Joe Tubby and I have now accomplished all of the goals which we set for ourselves at the beginning of the trip. We made detailed sketches at Smith's Lake, Racket Lake, Blue Mountain and Racket Falls. Along the way we camped out, boated and tramped along the road and on faint trails. We finished our sketches of the famous Indian Pass this past Monday and during the next two days we climbed Mount Tahawus, the tallest mountain in the state.

During that climb I twisted my knee when I slipped on a rock crossing a stream. This did not keep me from completing the climb, but as we descended the pain increased to the point I wondered if my companions would be required to carry me or leave me behind. As soon as I reached our tent, I wrapped my knee in a wet cloth and fell into an exhausted sleep.

My knee was quite swollen and painful to touch the next day. I needed to lay about camp resting it as the others rowed out in the lake to fish. In the afternoon Joe and his brother Josiah went down to the village, where they told everyone they met the story of our mountain adventure. At the post office they met Mrs. Ralph, the mother of one of the managers of the works, who fetched some liniment from home and sent it to me. I have been applying it liberally and it seems to be having a most satisfactory effect.

I was still lame yesterday and had to stay in camp resting. Joe and Josiah went to the village again in the morning, and when they returned at noon, they announced that they had decided to leave for home. They had already made arrangements to send their baggage to the Lower Works on the mail boat that same afternoon. When we finished our last dinner together, they busied themselves packing up their things.

We had agreed at the time Josiah joined us back at our Racket Lake camp that we would return home separately. Joe is needed in his father's business and Josiah naturally wanted to travel home with his elder brother. I had hoped that they both would remain with me until we could travel to the Schroon River together, but I appreciated their restlessness caused by sitting in camp with no goal other than awaiting my recovery.

When they finished packing their knapsacks, they took everything down to the boat we had borrowed. "Placing their things in this boat, Joe came up to me to give me his hand, and as I gave him the farewell grasp I felt a choking sensation, a deep emotion that I could with difficulty conceal. It was hard for me to part here in the edge of the wilderness whose depths we had treaded and whose discomforts we had borne together. I felt an affection for him at that moment that I never did before and I strove in vain to conceal my feelings of sorrow [at] parting with him. . . . All the way across we kept up a cheerful conversation of hearty farewells until they had gone too far to be heard. After landing, they bade Puffer goodbye and lingering as long as they could in sight, they waved their hats which I answered by waving mine in turn, and [after I climbed] up the bank the forest swallowed them from my sight."

My knee feels much better today. I spent the afternoon sketching in the village. I told Puffer that I would be ready to start preparations for our departure tomorrow. He went to the boardinghouse to check on some baggage we had stored there. When he returned, he handed me a note from Joe that said he and Josiah had stayed there last night and they didn't come back to camp because they didn't want to have to part again.

I hope you are keeping well. Please give my regards to your mother and father. I shall write you again after I reach home in a few weeks' time.

Sincerely, your friend,

Jervis

Notes for Letter 29

The trip journal makes it clear that the artists originally intended to leave for home as soon as possible after returning from their climb of Mount Marcy. McEntee's knee injury was serious enough, though, to prevent him from traveling. After idling in camp for two days, Joe and Josiah Tubby decided they would head home. They were planning to stay a day or two at Schroon River on the trip home, spend some time at Crown Point and Lake George, then continue home to Rondout. They thought this would take them about a week.

In the article that appeared in the *Lowville Northern Journal* on August 27, 1851, McEntee says that he planned to return to Lowville with Puffer to retrieve items they had left behind at the start of the trip.[1] Tubby's dog was also at Puffer's farm. Given that his article was written on July 24 while he was in the camp at Blue Mountain, it appears that McEntee and Tubby had already decided to return home separately long before they parted at their Henderson Lake camp.

One explanation for Tubby's need to return to Rondout ahead of McEntee is that he was probably needed at his father's business. Joe Tubby had probably begun to work for his father during his teens. He learned house painting, wallpapering, and sign painting. I imagine that in 1851, however, Joe Tubby was not yet employed full-time by his father since he was able to be absent for much of the summer. We know that by 1858 he had started to take a more active part in the business. He eventually specialized in the decorative painting popular at the time, trompe l'oeil, which made common wooden fittings appear to be marble or rare hardwoods. For the rest of his life, he worked full-time as a builder while creating a series of beautiful landscape paintings in his spare time.[2]

While camped at Henderson Lake, the group had the luxury of obtaining an almost daily supply of food from a (French) Canadian family who lived on the edge of the village. They were able to obtain

1. McEntee, "'Camp Church,' Ragged Lake, July 24, 1851."
2. See Levy, *Joseph Tubby*.

freshly baked bread, butter, milk, and other food that they were deprived of at their more remote campsites earlier in the trip. There
were several Canadian families living in the High Peaks area. Some
had come for logging jobs, and some for mining. As noted in the next
letter, a "reckless Canadian" drove McEntee and Puffer to the Schroon Valley when they departed from the mountains.

Starting Home

To Mr. & Mrs. James S. McEntee, Clovertop, Rondout, New York
Monday, August 18, 1851

Dear Father, dear Mother,

Puffer and I reached Root's Hotel at the Schroon River late this afternoon. We rode here in a very long and unyielding lumber wagon driven at breakneck speed over a rough corduroy road by a reckless Canadian. Puffer never complained during the journey, but after we arrived, he muttered it was the "cussedest travelin'" he had ever experienced. Here is my sketch of how I imagine we looked during our ride today.

We will depart here tomorrow after breakfast, bound for Lake George. From there we will make our way south to Albany and then travel west on the Erie Canal to Rome, where we can board the stage to Lowville. After visiting with attorney Sylvester, I will collect the things we left behind there and return home directly.

My last week in the Adirondacks proved a worthy conclusion to our adventure. Joe and I finished our sketches of the famous Indian Pass last Monday. This goal accomplished, we departed camp on Tuesday to climb Mount Tahawus, the tallest mountain in the state. It was my bad luck that while crossing a shallow stream during the ascent, my foot slipped and I wrenched my knee. I considered abandoning the climb but decided the pain was not so severe as to prevent me from continuing. We reached the summit early the next morning. As we descended the mountain the pain increased considerably. I was having some trouble walking by the time we reached our camp at Henderson Lake. The next day I was fortunate to receive a gift of some liniment from Mrs. Ralph, the mother of the mine supervisor.

VOL. I.—23.

THE CANADIAN'S TEAM.

3.4. Jervis McEntee, *The Canadian's Team*, wood engraving by Loomis-Annin from sketch by Jervis McEntee. In McEntee, "The Lakes of the Wilderness," 349. Courtesy of the American Antiquarian Society, Worcester, MA.

I resolved to apply the salve frequently and rest in camp until my knee mended.

I assume you are already aware of the fact that Joe and Josiah departed from camp together this past Friday bound for home. I was sad to see them go, but I appreciated their restlessness caused by sitting in camp with no goal other than awaiting my recovery.

By Saturday the pain in my knee had receded enough that I was able to go down to the village with Puffer to do some sketching and to thank Mrs. Ralph for the liniment. I had a nice talk with her and showed her some of my sketches, which she greatly admired. She has a surprisingly keen eye for art that she attributes to her frequent discussions with her son, who has an interest in landscape painting and does some painting of mountain scenes for his own amusement.

While walking about the village, I had the good fortune to meet a local man named Thompson who was with Headley on Tahawus when he visited here a few years ago. Thompson remembers Headley vividly and left me with the distinct impression that Headley's book exaggerated the facts of his climb to cast Headley in a better light than what Thompson recalls. I also briefly met the son of Henderson, the former superintendent, who's sad ending I related in a previous letter.

I was still feeling somewhat tired yesterday but I was determined to depart camp for home. I dispatched Puffer to the village to find someone willing to drive us and our baggage to Root's, a trip of about thirty miles on the road. I was still resting when Puffer returned and started to cook our dinner. The savory odor of roasting trout finally roused me. Puffer reported that he had engaged a wagon and driver. The rest of the afternoon found us packing to prepare for an early departure. I will write you again soon to let you know of my progress towards home.

Your obedient son,
Jervis

Notes for Letter 30

McEntee's trip journal ends abruptly midway through Sunday, August 17, with an observation about Puffer trapping a ground squirrel. I carefully examined the handwritten copy of the journal for any indication of why it contains no record of the rest of the trip. The last entry is followed by a page in different handwriting containing a list of what appear to be purchases, possibly from a feed store. No pages appear to have been removed from the bound volume. Perhaps McEntee miscalculated the number of pages needed to transcribe his journal, ran out of space in the bound volume, and completed his narrative elsewhere. If he did so, that remainder has been lost.

McEntee's account of the end of the trip that appears in "The Lakes of the Wilderness" (1859) contains two further interesting details: a ride in a lumber wagon from the High Peaks to the Schroon Valley and a claim that he and Tubby constructed a makeshift statue before departing.

The story of the uncomfortable ride in a lumber wagon from the Upper Works to the Schroon River Valley and its illustration are detailed enough to be true. McEntee and Puffer reached the Schroon River at the end of a long day, so I surmise that they stayed at least one night at Root's Hotel, located there along the road, since it was a known waypoint in 1851 where transportation could be obtained to Crown Point on Lake Champlain or to Lake George. Unfortunately, the story told in "The Lakes" ends without giving an account of how McEntee and Puffer traveled the rest of the way home.

The best evidence for the remainder of the trip is found in McEntee's article published in the *Lowville Northern Journal* on August 27, 1851.[1] There he says his plan was to pass through the Schroon Valley, go to Lake George, then return to Lowville via Whitehall, Albany, and Utica. Some of that trip would be by boat, and some by stage. McEntee planned to pick up the baggage left behind at the start of the trip and presumably Tubby's dog. He would likely have returned

---

1. McEntee, "'Camp Church,' Ragged Lake, July 24, 1851."

THE GENIUS LOCI

3.5. Jervis McEntee, *The Genius Loci*, wood engraving by Loomis-Annin from sketch by Jervis McEntee. In McEntee, "The Lakes of the Wilderness," 349. Courtesy of the American Antiquarian Society, Worcester, MA.

to Rondout by reversing course to Rome by stage, to Albany by boat on the Erie Canal, then back down the Hudson to Rondout. He was probably back home by the end of August.

McEntee also claims in "The Lakes" that before he and Tubby left their camp at Henderson Lake, they assembled a statue he called the *Genius Loci*. In the article, he included an etching that shows the sculpture perched on a windswept rock and the artists saluting it from the lower-left corner as they depart. McEntee's initials are worked discretely into the front edge of the rock.

McEntee had studied Latin in school and loved to sprinkle his writing with references to classical literature. In Roman religion, the genius loci was the protective spirit of a particular place. By McEntee's time, the phrase had come to mean the distinctive impression that a particular place creates in one's mind.

McEntee described the statue this way: "From a pair of wretchedly dilapidated boots, worn out on weary forest marches, a pair of pantaloons torn and riddled in the Tahawus expedition, an old sketching umbrella and a frying pan, we constructed a statue, which we inaugurated as the *genius loci* for all who come after us to honor and respect."[2] The items they used to fashion the statue symbolize four significant aspects of their Adirondack experience. The tattered sketching umbrella represents the many days he and Tubby spent sketching in hard-to-reach wild places. The frying pan represents the challenges and rewards of obtaining food during the trip. The torn pantaloons are a reminder of the successful but difficult and painful climb of Mount Marcy, an event that McEntee saw as the climax of the trip. The boots represent the many miles he slogged along rough trails in his inadequate and constantly deteriorating boots.

By placing the statue story at the conclusion of his trip account in "The Lakes," McEntee emphasized the lasting effect that the sketching trip had on him. The magazine article and its engravings were, after all, created seven or eight years after the trip. In crafting his conclusion to the tale, he wanted to create an illustration that encapsulated what he most remembered: the constant preoccupation with food, the trouble they went to in service of art, the climb up Mount Marcy, and his ragged boots. The statue not only captures all these things but also highlights the fact that by the time McEntee left for home, he felt that the distinctive spirit of the wild Adirondacks had firmly established itself in his soul.

2. McEntee, "The Lakes of the Wilderness," 350.

Concluding Remarks

One clear outcome of the sketching trip in 1851 was that both Mc-
Entee and Tubby had convinced themselves that they deserved to be
regarded as serious artists. The trip proved that they were physically
and mentally able to devote a whole summer to their art. McEntee's
journal makes it clear that they enjoyed the process immensely despite
the occasional hardship. Importantly, they learned to see a genuine
wilderness landscape in ways only an artist understands. They spent
hours, even days, drawing and redrawing what they saw until they felt
they had captured its essence. That process is what convinced them
that they had within themselves the skill and the vision to create beautiful works of art.

According to McEntee's trip journal, he and Tubby returned with
their sketching boxes full of preliminary pencil drawings as well as
several more detailed painted sketches that they clearly intended to
transform into finished paintings. Some of these painted sketches,
such as the ones they made at Smith's Lake, Raquette Falls, and the
Indian Pass, must have been quite elaborate because they took as long
as four full days of constant work to complete.

In 1852, the year after the trip, McEntee and Tubby exhibited at
the National Academy of Design two finished oil paintings each derived from their Adirondack sketches. McEntee showed *A View in the
Forest of Northern New York—Outlet of Smith's Lake* and *Saw Mill at
the Adirondac Iron Works*. Tubby exhibited *Landscape, Adirondac* and
Landscape, Indian Pass in the Adirondac.[1] There does not appear to have

---

1. These four paintings are listed in *National Academy of Design Exhibition Record, 1826–1860*, comp. Bartlett Cowdrey, 2:15 (McEntee paintings), 2:167 (Tubby
paintings).

been any published reviews of these paintings. If these four paintings survive, their current whereabouts are unknown.

Most of the many sketches they made have disappeared or are unidentified. The only original pencil sketch made during the trip in a public collection now is the one McEntee made of Wood's cabin at Raquette Lake.[2] A rough sketch of Puffer cooking a trout precedes the first page of McEntee's handwritten trip journal. McEntee probably made this sketch from memory at the time he copied the journal into the bound volume now in the collection of The Adirondack Experience.

McEntee's color sketch of Blue Mountain from Raquette Lake was once in the private collection of Warder Cadbury, an early research associate at the Adirondack Museum who discovered most of the items that form the McEntee Papers at the Archives of American Art in the Smithsonian. A copy of that sketch appears on the cover of Barbara McMartin's book *To the Lake of the Skies* (1996). A copy of the wood engraving of that same scene appears here with letter 16 of July 14 (figure 2.4). Cadbury also once owned Tubby's sketch of Blue Mountain made the same day, and that sketch appears as the frontispiece of McMartin's book. The current whereabouts of these two works is unknown.

A large collection of McEntee's sketches was purchased by his friend the artist Lockwood De Forest, but a catalog of those sketches does not include any from the 1851 trip.[3] A search of the collection catalogs of the museums holding works by McEntee and Tubby has not turned up any of the other sketches made by either artist during the trip. I strongly suspect, however, that some may still exist in private collections.

For many years after the trip, McEntee continued to paint Adirondack scenes. In 1855, four years after the trip, he produced his

2. This sketch is in the collection of The Adirondack Experience, The Museum on Blue Mountain Lake, and is reproduced in Mandel, *Fair Wilderness*, 147.

3. See Sandra Kay Feldman, curator, *A Selection of Drawings from the Lockwood de Forest Collection*, catalog, exhibition May 4–28, 1976 (New York: Hirschl & Adler Galleries, 1976).

beautiful *Study for Adirondack Woods*. This painting, likely based on a sketch done in the summer of 1851, is now in a private collection.[4]

In 1858–59, seven years after the trip, McEntee commissioned eighteen wood engravings based on his sketches from 1851. These engravings, copies of which appear in this book, were used as illustrations for McEntee's unsigned story "The Lakes of the Wilderness," published in the *Great Republic Monthly* on April 1, 1859.

From surviving correspondence in the Archives of American Art, we know McEntee returned to the Adirondacks in the fall of 1863 with his friends and fellow artists Sanford Robinson Gifford and Richard William Hubbard. Together they visited Lake George, the Champlain Valley, the High Peaks, Lake Placid, and Blue Mountain Lake. There is at least one surviving finished painting by McEntee from this trip, titled *Near Bolton, Lake George*.[5] A faint pencil sketch of Lake George (with the date "Sept. 10, 1863" inscribed on the back) is in the collection of Vassar College.[6] Following the trip in 1863, McEntee completed a painting of the view from the summit of Mount Marcy titled *Mount Tahawas—Adirondacks*.

McEntee and Gifford returned to the Adirondacks in August–September 1866 with Gifford's sister Mary and McEntee's wife, Gertrude. McEntee's sketchbook from this trip is in the collection of the Detroit Institute of Arts. Based on the dates on the sketches, during that trip they again climbed Mount Marcy by approaching it from Keene Valley and the Ausable Lakes. McEntee also painted a view of Whiteface Mountain as seen from Lake Placid on that trip.

4. A reproduction of that painting can be found in Vedder, *Jervis McEntee*, 56, and in Jane E. Egan, *McEntee & Company*, catalog, exhibition Nov. 25, 1997–Jan. 17, 1998 (New York: Beacon Hill Fine Art, 1997), plate 10, p. 22.

5. A reproduction can be found in Debra Force and Elizabeth Hendry, curators, *A Diary Illuminated: Oil Sketches by Jervis McEntee*, catalog, exhibition Nov. 12–Dec. 21, 2007 (New York: Debra Force Fine Art, 2007), 6–7.

6. This pencil sketch can be viewed on the Vassar museum's online site at https://emuseum.vassar.edu/collections.

McEntee showed some of his recent Adirondack paintings at the annual exhibitions of the National Academy of Design. He showed *Study in a Hemlock Wood* in 1856, *Mount Tahawas—Adirondacks* in 1863, and *Lake Placid—Adirondac Mts.* in 1868. As noted earlier, *Hemlock Wood* still exists in a private collection. *Lake Placid* is in the collection of the Minnesota Marine Art Museum in Winona. The whereabouts of *Mount Tahawas* is unknown, but an interesting description of that painting appears in Henry T. Tuckerman's *Book of the Artists* (1867):

> His "Mount Tahawas" is not adequately luminous in tone, but its conception shows a certain experimental courage which is auspicious; it represents a mountain at the moment of early day, when the mist begins to roll in great drifts away from its summit. Whoever has watched the freaks of the mist in the heart of a mountainous region, will find some touches in this picture true to nature and rarely reproduced; others may strike him as apocryphal; but, in the freedom and novelty of the treatment, we find another evidence of the untraditional, confidently sympathetic spirit in which our landscape-artists look at nature.[7]

In addition, an undated pencil sketch titled *Mist on the Mountains* is in the collection of the Art Institute of Chicago. It resembles McEntee's other sketches from the Adirondack High Peaks trip of 1866 but cannot be definitively linked to that trip. A small undated oil painting titled *Mountain Mist in the Morning* was sold by the auction house James D. Julia, Inc., on February 2, 2012, and is presumably now in a private collection.[8] This painting could possibly be McEntee's painted sketch of the Indian Pass as it bears a close resemblance to Thomas Cole's sketches and Ingham's painting of the pass.

7. Henry T. Tuckerman, "Landscape Painters," in *Book of the Artists: American Artist Life, Comprising Biographical and Critical Sketches of American Artists: Preceded by an Historical Account of the Rise and Progress of Art in America* (New York: Putnam, 1867), 543.

8. Information about this painting and other McEntee paintings sold at auction was found through the art auction website Invaluable. The original auction house that sold the painting has since been acquired by a larger competitor.

There is no evidence that McEntee returned to the Adirondacks after 1866. Available lists of exhibitions in which McEntee participated and recent exhibit catalogs of McEntee's work do not include any other paintings or sketches with a detectable Adirondack connection. Nonetheless, there can be no doubt that McEntee had once intended Adirondack landscapes to be a significant part of his artistic portfolio for at least fifteen years after the sketching trip he took in 1851. Indeed, when the writer Thomas Bailey Aldrich visited McEntee in his New York City studio in 1866, he noted that the studio was "filled" with sketches from the Catskills and the Adirondacks.[9]

For his part, Joseph Tubby did not devote much attention to Adirondack subjects. Aside from the two paintings exhibited at the National Academy of Design in 1852 mentioned earlier, Tubby appears not to have painted any further Adirondack scenes until 1894–95, when he completed a small oil painting of Star Lake. It is unknown when or if he visited Star Lake to sketch this scene, but he died soon after creating the painting, in 1896. This painting is in the collection of The Adirondack Experience, The Museum on Blue Mountain Lake.[10]

It's interesting to speculate why Tubby did not do more with his hard-earned Adirondack sketches. It seems most likely that economics was a significant factor. Tubby was never able to devote himself to his art full-time. To make a living, he continued to work as a building contractor. He married in 1858 and had six children. Since he was able to paint only in his spare time, the number of paintings he could produce was limited. He loved landscape painting, but there were not many opportunities to sell his paintings in Kingston. Because of these factors, his later paintings were mostly scenes of the Hudson River Valley and Catskills near his home.[11]

McEntee faced economic problems of a different sort. Immediately after the trip in 1851, he went to work in his uncle's feed store

9. T. B. Aldrich, "Among the Studios," *Our Young Folks: An Illustrated Magazine for Boys and Girls* 2, no. 10 (Oct. 1866): 624–25.

10. Mandel, *Fair Wilderness*, plate 319.

11. Levy, *Joseph Tubby*, 6–14.

and painted in his spare time. He was able, however, to use his contacts in New York City to sell enough paintings that he could stop working in the store by 1855. He married in 1854 and built a studio home in Rondout. By 1857, he had a studio in New York City as well as the one in Rondout. For many years, he was productive, and his paintings sold well, but judging from his later journals, money was always a concern.[12]

Based on contemporary reviews of his work, I believe McEntee increasingly chose to paint scenes set in the Hudson Valley because those paintings had become commercially popular.[13] He gradually began to specialize in paintings set in the fall and winter. His distinctive choice of fall and winter scenes for his later paintings has contributed to the view that he had a melancholy personality. This view was expressed often enough in reviews that he wrote a letter to William George Sheldon in 1879 to refute it: "Some people call my landscapes gloomy and disagreeable. They say I paint the sorrowful side of nature. . . . But this is a mistake. . . . Nature is not sad to me but quiet, pensive, restful."[14]

Biographies of McEntee and Tubby largely ignore their Adirondack trip. This neglect is understandable. As just detailed, neither artist took much effort to preserve the Adirondack sketches they labored so mightily to create. Neither publicly credited the trip as a significant influence on their later work. Although McEntee appears to have once intended to publicize the trip by writing an illustrated magazine article, for some reason he eventually chose to publish this article

12. The facts of McEntee's life given here are drawn from the numerous secondary sources about McEntee listed in the section "Secondary Sources about McEntee" in "Sources Consulted" at the back of the book. The most comprehensive of these accounts is Thing, *The Street That Built a City*, 43–90.

13. Contemporary assessments of McEntee's art are included in each of the catalogs that accompanied recent exhibits of his work. See this list in the "Exhibit Catalogs" section of "Sources Consulted."

14. "Letter from Jervis McEntee to William George Sheldon, 1879," printed in full in Vedder, *Jervis McEntee*, 10–11.

anonymously. Even though economic forces directed both McEntee and Tubby away from painting many Adirondack scenes, I believe it was the sketching trip of 1851 that confirmed their respective artistic callings.

McEntee had a very successful career as a landscape artist. He was able to make painting his full-time occupation for most of his adult life. For a time, he was probably among the top-ten Hudson River School painters in terms of successful sales, number of works in museum collections, durability and longevity in the movement, commitment to art as a profession, and general capability as an artist. The fact that McEntee had some financial advantages at the start of his career and that, unlike Tubby, he had no children does not diminish his success.

The same natural forces that drew McEntee and Tubby to the central Adirondacks are stronger than ever these days. Throngs of visitors come to the Adirondacks to experience the mixture of outdoor adventure and sublime beauty that so attracted McEntee and Tubby. We still camp out, sometimes in an Adirondack lean-to, hike the trails, paddle the lakes and rivers, and climb the mountains. We still stand in wonder at the Indian Pass and on the summit of Mount Marcy. We brave the bugs and the sudden thunderstorms. We enjoy reflections on a still lake and the wild call of the loon. At the spots where McEntee and Tubby spent hours sketching, we stop, pause for a moment, and take a photograph.

McEntee and Tubby were among a very small handful of early Adirondack tourists who came to the great north woods primarily seeking beauty and tranquility. Over the intervening years, their romantic vision of the Adirondacks has gained legions of adherents. Millions have followed in their faint footsteps without ever knowing that these artists passed this way long ago.

Acknowledgments

Sources Consulted

Index

Acknowledgments

I first read the Jervis McEntee trip journal for 1851 in April 2016 at the suggestion of Mary Kunzler-Larmann, a devotee of Adirondack history who has a camp at Beaver River, New York. She strongly urged me to read it because of its vivid description of the Adirondacks before any appreciable development had occurred. I took her suggestion and was captured by the language and amazed at the audacity of the trip. As this project advanced through various stages, Mary served as the first reader of the draft manuscript. Without her encouragement, this book would not exist.

Once there was a complete draft of the manuscript, I had the good fortune to obtain the assistance of Lowell Thing, whose expert knowledge of the life and art of Jervis McEntee was invaluable. The finished book owes a great deal to his helpful editorial comments.

Ivy Gocker, the former librarian at the research library of The Adirondack Experience, The Museum on Blue Mountain Lake, made it possible for me to closely examine McEntee's handwritten trip journal and helped me search the collection for related manuscript material. Ms. Gocker also put me in touch with Don Seauvageau, the president of the Newcomb Historical Museum Board of Trustees. He freely shared insights from his research as well as a draft of a section of his revised Town of Newcomb history devoted to McEntee's trip.

A draft of the full manuscript was workshopped during the Colgate Writers' Conference of 2022 in a session led by Gregory Bottoms, professor of English and codirector of the Reporting and Documentary Storytelling Minor at the University of Vermont. The other writers who participated in the workshop were Jennifer Benson, Christy Dittrick, Alison Fromme, Caroline Hurwitz, and David Johnson. Friends also read sections of the manuscript at various points and offered their encouragement, criticism, and helpful suggestions. I thank Dennis Buckley, Noel Sherry, Harmon

Hoff, Chris Rossi, John Bailey, Margo Thompson, Allison Woeger, and Jim Leiter.

Laura Fish, my editor at Syracuse University Press, guided the manuscript through the revision process and advocated for the project to the faculty editorial board. She helped me find ways to make a compelling case for the story with prospective readers.

This book owes a great deal to support and encouragement from my wife, Meredith Leonard. She willingly discussed the project with me as I wrestled the story into shape, and she helped point out areas that needed clarification. In so many ways, she accompanied me as I walked across the Adirondacks beside Jervis, Joe, Josiah, and Puffer.

Sources Consulted

Works by Jervis McEntee

Jervis McEntee Papers, 1796, 1848–1905. Archives of American Art, Smithsonian Institution, Washington, DC. Contains a copy of the journal of 1851 and its transcript; miscellaneous letters and other writings unrelated to the Adirondack sketching trip; five volumes of McEntee's later journals, digitized with transcripts, covering from May 10, 1872, to November 1, 1890.

McEntee, Jervis. "Address." In *Sanford Gifford Memorial Meeting of the Century Association*, 49–57. New York: Century Association, 1880.

———— [J. M.]. "'Camp Church,' Ragged Lake, July 24, 1851." *Lowville Northern Journal*, Aug. 20 and 27, 1851. Copy and typescript of the complete article is in the research library of The Adirondack Experience, The Museum on Blue Mountain Lake, Blue Mountain Lake, NY.

————. Jervis McEntee Diary, August 1844–October 1845. Special Collections Research Center, Syracuse Univ. Libraries, Syracuse, NY.

————. "Jervis McEntee, a Journal of Facts, Folly and Fun, 1845–1846." Department of Special Collections and University Archives, McFarlin Library, Univ. of Tulsa, Tulsa, OK.

————. "John Vanderlyn." *Putnam's Monthly Magazine* 3 (June 1854): 593–95.

————. "Journal of the 1851 Adirondack Sketching Trip." MS 67-019. Research library of The Adirondack Experience, The Museum on Blue Mountain Lake, Blue Mountain Lake, NY. Contains both the original handwritten, bound journal and a typed transcript.

———— [no byline]. "The Lakes of the Wilderness." *Great Republic Monthly*, Apr. 1, 1859, 335–50. Illustrated article.

———— [J. M.]. "Rambles in the Adirondacks." *Rondout Courier*, July 18, 1851.

————. "Reminiscences of Vanderlyn." *The Crayon* 3 (Mar. 1856): 89–90.

McEntee, Jervis, and Waldo Pratt, eds. *A Memorial Catalogue of the Paintings of Sanford Robinson Gifford*. New York: Metropolitan Museum of Art, 1881.

Exhibit Catalogs and Reproductions of McEntee's Art

Bryant, William Cullen. *Among the Trees*. Illustrated with designs by Jervis McEntee, engraved by Harley. New York: Putnam, 1874.

Egan, Jane E. *McEntee & Company*. Catalog, exhibition Nov. 25, 1997–Jan. 17, 1998. New York: Beacon Hill Fine Art, 1997. Includes an essay by J. Gray Sweeney.

Feldman, Sandra Kay, curator. *A Selection of Drawings from the Lockwood de Forest Collection*. Catalog, exhibition May 4–28, 1976. New York: Hirschl & Adler Galleries, 1976.

Force, Debra, and Elizabeth Hendry, curators. *A Diary Illuminated: Oil Sketches by Jervis McEntee*. Catalog, exhibition Nov. 12–Dec. 21, 2007. New York: Debra Force Fine Art, 2007.

Thing, Lowell, curator. *Jervis McEntee: Kingston's Artist of the Hudson River School*. Catalog, exhibition May 1–Oct. 15, 2015. Kingston, NY: Friends of Historic Kingston, 2015.

Vedder, Lee E., curator. *Jervis McEntee: Painter-Poet of the Hudson River School*. Catalog, exhibition Aug. 25–Dec. 13, 2015. New Paltz, NY: Samuel Dorsky Museum of Art, State Univ. of New York, 2015. Includes essays by Kerry Dean Carso and David Schuyler.

Secondary Sources about McEntee

Aldrich, T. B. [Thomas Bailey]. "Among the Studios." *Our Young Folks: An Illustrated Magazine for Boys and Girls* 2, no. 10 (Oct. 1866): 624–25.

"American Painters—Jervis McEntee." *Art Journal* 2 (1876): 178–79.

Avery, Kevin J. "Jervis McEntee." In *American National Biography*, vol. 15, 33–35. Oxford: Oxford Univ. Press, 1999.

Cadbury, Warder H. "The Adirondack Bookshelf." *The Adirondac*, Mar.–Apr. 1964, 28–29.

1892 Century Association Yearbook. New York: Century Association, 1892.

Schuyler, David. "Jervis McEntee: The Trials of a Landscape Painter." In *The Cultured Canvas: New Perspectives on American Landscape Painting*, edited by Nancy Siegel, 185–216. Durham, NH: Univ. of New Hampshire Press, 2011.

———. *Sanctified Landscape: Writers, Artists, and the Hudson River Valley, 1820–1909*. Ithaca, NY: Cornell Univ. Press, 2012.

Thing, Lowell. *The Street That Built a City: McEntee's Chestnut Street, Kingston, and the Rise of New York*. Delmar, NY: Black Dome Press, 2015.

Tuckerman, Henry T. [Theodore]. "Landscape Painters." In *Book of the Artists: American Artist Life, Comprising Biographical and Critical Sketches Of American Artists: Preceded by an Historical Account of the Rise and Progress of Art in America*, 543–46. New York: Putnam, 1867.

Sources for Joseph Tubby and Julia McEntee Dillon

Glasner, Charles, and Sanford A. Levy, curators. *Julia McEntee Dillon: A Retrospective*. Catalog, exhibition May–Oct. 2005. Kingston, NY: Friends of Historic Kingston, 2005.

Joseph Tubby Papers, 1851–88. Microfilm roll 9, frames 339–561. Archives of American Art, Smithsonian Institution, Washington, DC. Contains two letters written by Tubby during the sketching trip of 1851 and miscellaneous other material unrelated to the trip.

Levy, Sanford A., curator. *Joseph Tubby, 1861–1896, Artist, Rondout, New York*. Catalog, exhibition May–Oct. 2008. Kingston, NY: Friends of Historic Kingston, 2008.

Other Sources

Ancestry.com. 1850 United States Federal Census (online database), 2009. https://www.ancestry.com/search/collections/8054/.

Avery, Kevin J. "Thomas Cole (1801–1848)." Aug. 2009. Heilbrunn Timeline of Art History, Metropolitan Museum of Art. http://www.metmuseum .org/toah/hd/cole/hd_cole.htm.

Bartlett Cowdrey, Mary, comp. *National Academy of Design Exhibition Record, 1826–1860*. 2 vols. New York: New York Historical Society, 1943.

Beach, Nelson. "Journal of Proceedings Relative to the Carthage and Lake Champlain Road." Apr. 14–June 16, 1841. Transcription by Noel Sherry. Collection of the Lewis County Historical Society, Lowville, NY.

Cole, Thomas. "Essay on American Scenery." *American Monthly Magazine* 1 (Jan. 1836): 1–12.

DeCosta, B. F. *Lake George: Its Scenes and Characteristics, with Glimpses of the Olden Times. To Which Is Added Some Account of Ticonderoga, with a*

Description of the Route to Schroon Lake and the Adirondacks. With . . . Notes on Lake Champlain. New York: A. D. F. Randolph, 1868.

Donaldson, Alfred L. *A History of the Adirondacks.* 1921. Unabridged reprint. Fleischmanns, NY: Purple Mountain Press, 1996.

Emmons, Ebenezer. *New York State Natural History Survey Report.* Albany: State of New York, 1838.

Goodwin, Tony, and David Thomas-Train, eds. *High Peaks Trails.* 14th ed. Lake George, NY: Adirondack Mountain Club, 2012.

Grady, Joseph F. *The Adirondacks, Fulton Chain–Big Moose Region: The Story of a Wilderness.* 3rd ed. Utica, NY: North Country, 1972.

Harvey, Eleanor Jones. *The Painted Sketch: American Impressions from Nature, 1830–1880.* Dallas: Dallas Museum of Art, Henry N. Abrams, 1998.

Headley, Joel T. *The Adirondack; Or, Life in the Woods.* 1849. Reprinted with an introduction by Philip G. Terrie. Bovina Center, NY: Harbor Hill, 1982.

Hildreth, Sandra. "Finding 'The Great Adirondack Pass.'" *Adirondack Almanack*, Apr. 5, 2012. https://www.adirondackalmanack.com/2012/04/sandy-hildreth-finding-the-great-adirondack-pass.html.

Hoffman, C. F. [Charles Fenno]. *Wild Scenes in the Forest and Prairie.* 2 vols. London: Richard Bentley, 1839.

Hough, Franklin B. *History of Lewis County, New York, with Illustrations and Biographical Sketches of Some of Its Prominent Men and Pioneers.* Syracuse, NY: Mason, 1883.

Jamieson, Paul, with Neal Burdick, eds. *The Adirondack Reader: Four Centuries of Adirondack Writing.* 3rd ed. Lake George, NY: Adirondack Mountain Club, 2009.

Kaiser, Harvey H. *Great Camps of the Adirondacks* (1982). Rev. ed. Jaffrey, NH: David R. Godine, 2020.

Lossing, Benson J. *The Hudson from the Wilderness to the Sea.* 1866. Reprint. Somersworth, NH: New Hampshire Publishing, 1972.

Mandel, Patricia C. F. *Fair Wilderness: American Paintings in the Collection of the Adirondack Museum.* Blue Mountain Lake, NY: Adirondack Museum, 1990.

Marshall, George. "Adirondack Guides of the High Peaks." In *The Adirondack High Peaks and the Forty-Sixers*, edited by Grace Hudowalski, 105–31. Albany, NY: Peters Print, 1970.

Masten, Arthur H. *The Story of Adirondac*. Syracuse, NY: Syracuse Univ. Press, 1968.

Masters, Raymond D. *A Social History of the Huntington Wildlife Forest*. Utica, NY: North Country, 1993.

McMartin, Barbara. *To the Lake of the Skies: The Benedicts in the Adirondacks*. Chicago: Lakeview Press, 1996.

Montgomery, Gladys. *An Elegant Wilderness: Great Camps and Grand Lodges of the Adirondacks, 1855–1935*. New York: Acanthus Press, 2011.

Naylor, Maria, comp. *National Academy of Design Exhibition Record, 1861–1900*. New York: Kennedy Galleries, 1973.

Noble, Louis Legrand. *The Life and Works of Thomas Cole*. 1964. Reprint. Hendersonville, NY: Black Dome Press, 1997.

Otis, Melissa. *Rural Indigenousness: A History of Iroquoian and Algonquian Peoples of the Adirondacks*. Syracuse, NY: Syracuse Univ. Press, 2018.

Pilcher, Edith. *The Constables, First Family of the Adirondacks*. Utica, NY: North Country, 1992.

Pitts, Edward I. *Beaver River Country: An Adirondack History*. Syracuse, NY: Syracuse Univ. Press, 2022.

Potter, Orlando B., III, and Donald Brandreth Potter. *Brandreth: A Band of Cousins Preserves the Oldest Adirondack Family Enclave*. Utica, NY: North Country, 2011.

Prescott, Mike. "Ferrand Benedict's Abandoned Newcomb–Long Lake Canal." *Adirondack Almanack*, June 11, 2016. https://www.adirondack almanack.com/2016/06/short-biography-farrad-benedict-conclusion.html.

Prince, J. Dyneley. "Some Forgotten Indian Place-Names in the Adirondacks." *Journal of American Folk-Lore*, Apr. 1900, 123–28.

Raymond, Henry J. "A Week in the Wilderness." *New York Daily Times*, 1855. Reprinted in Harold K. Hochschild, *Township #34: A History with Digressions of an Adirondack Township in Hamilton County in the State of New York*, addendum to chap. 13, 170–75. New York: Published by the author, 1952.

Sasso, John. "Historical Profile—Blue Mountain: Beyond the Fire Tower." History and Legends of the Adirondacks, Facebook group, Nov. 27, 2017. https://www.facebook.com/groups/adirondackhistory/.

Schreier, Philip. "History of the Hunting Rifle in America." *American Hunter* (NRA), May 16, 2015. https://www.americanhunter.org/content/history -of-the-hunting-rifle-in-america/.

Smith, H. Perry. *History of Essex County*. Syracuse, NY: D. Mason, 1885.

————. *Modern Babes in the Woods; Or, Summerings in the Wilderness. To Which Is Added a Reliable and Descriptive Guide to the Adirondacks by E. R. Wallace*. Hartford, CT: Columbian Book, 1872.

Stephens, W. Hudson. *Historical Notes of the Settlement on No. 4, Brown's Tract, in Watson, Lewis County, N.Y. with Notices of the Early Settlers*. Utica, NY: Roberts, 1864.

Stoddard, Seneca Ray. *The Adirondacks, Illustrated*. Albany, NY: Weed, Parsons, 1874.

Street, Alfred Billings. *The Indian Pass*. 1869. Facsimile reprint. Fleischmanns, NY: Purple Mountain Press, 1993.

Sulavik, Stephen B. *The Adirondack Guideboat: Its Origins, Its Builders, and Their Boats*. With revisions and additions by Edward Comstock Jr. and Christopher H. Woodward. Peterborough, NH: Bauhan, 2018.

Sylvester, Nathaniel Bartlett. *Historical Sketches of Northern New York and the Adirondack Wilderness, Etc.* 1877. Reprint, Peru, NY: Bloated Toe, 2014.

————. *The History of Ulster County with Illustrations and Biographical Sketches of Its Prominent Men and Pioneers*. Philadelphia: Everts & Peck, 1880.

Terrie, Philip G. *Wildlife and Wilderness: A History of Adirondack Mammals*. Bovina Center, NY: Purple Mountain Press, 1993.

Thacher, Tom. *Fifty Acres of Beach and Wood*. Raquette Lake, NY: Birch Point Press, 2016.

Thompson, H. H. [Henry Hunn]. "On the Wilderness Trail." *Forest and Stream* 7, no. 8 (Sept. 28, 1876): 114.

Todd, John, DD. *Summer Gleanings: Or, Sketches and Incidents of a Pastor's Vacation*. Northampton, MA: Hopkins, Bridgman, 1852.

Wallace, Edwin R. *Descriptive Guide to the Adirondacks: And Handbook of Travel to Saratoga Springs, Schroon Lake, Lakes Luzerne, George, and Champlain, the Ausable Chasm, the Thousand Islands, Massena Springs and Trenton Falls*. Hartford, CT: Columbian Book, 1872. This book's later editions were published by W. Gill, Syracuse, NY, the last one in 1897.

Weber, Sandra. *Mount Marcy: The High Peak of New York*. Fleischmanns, NY: Purple Mountain Press, 2001.

Index

Edward I. Pitts is a retired attorney and former Social Security administrative law judge who lives in Syracuse, New York. His book *Beaver River Country: An Adirondack History* was published by Syracuse University Press in 2022. His articles on Adirondack history have appeared in *Adirondack Life*, *Adirondac*, *LOCALadk*, the *Adirondack Almanack* (online), and the *New York Almanack* (online). He also maintains a blog of short, illustrated articles titled *Annals of the Beaver River*. He is a regular contributor to the Facebook group History and Legends of the Adirondacks. He is a member of the Rap-Shaw Club on Stillwater Reservoir and served as the president of its board of directors from 2011 to 2016. Before becoming a lawyer, he taught philosophy at St. Bonaventure University and Pennsylvania State University.